Let The Dead Man Walk

ISBN: 0-9715539-0-4

ANSELM
ANYOHA, MD.

LET THE DEAD
MAN WALK
PATIENTS BLUES
DOCTORS DELUSION

A NOVEL

2003

Let The Dead Man Walk

ACKNOWLEDGEMENT

Acknowledgement goes to a large number of people. First to my wife Sandra who assured me that I have a credible story to tell and motivated me to get this manuscript published. And to my ten years old son Rockwell, my nephew Benvin who had the misfortune but yet the enthusiasm to read back to me the earlier first few chapters of the manuscript. To my sister Olive who kept re-enkindling my zeal by asking numerous times, "Is your book published yet?" To numerous friends and relations who helped with the tedious task of editing a Physicians manuscript. On this note my appreciation goes to: Stephanie, Amy, Brian, and many others who chose to be anonymous.

When a free thinking African born Doctor graduated from medical school he set out to pursue his childhood desire. To dealt the final blow to the death coffin. To let the dead man walk again by using the untapped energies of 'The Breath' channeled through a device that would be known as 'inspigorate'. But that was only the beginning of his grope in the darkness of mortality. From his tiny village in Burundu, his determination drove him to the New World where there is no limit to human dream. For months his attitude and mannerism had to endure scores of patients cynicisms in a tough medical culture of the Bronx Borough. Engulfed in a capital cloud his dream soon became relegated to the back burner. Could anyone else rescue his mission before it flicks out? To his dismay he was going to fight death all by himself. All that changed when he met an Engineer willing to take a crack at his idea. It is insightful, doable, frightful, imaginative and fun as the Author nibble's at the possibilities and shakes up the medical status quo.

*To my grandma,Elizabeth Anyoha who died in 1981
just months after I entered medical school. And to all my
deceased patients especially those who were less prepared
and less priviledged to fight death*

1.

Except for the refilling clicks and rumbles of the aging respirator the theater was agonizingly tranquil. Stripped of the usual sporadic banters, silly jokes, salivary cheers, and verbal diarrhea spilling from the wet tongues of ancillary sycophants. All fun, all craziness seemed to have abated like a windless summer afternoon abruptly replacing the breezy evening fall.

In this same theater many years ago everybody was falling on each other's lap wiggling with laughter. Tickling at the slightest provocation. But then the atmosphere was friendly different. Though resources where not in abundance, essential instruments were not lacking. The air moved freely and so were spoken words amidst other regular activities. There were indeed several regular activities.

Laboring mothers pre-determined to be capable of natural delivery were expected to patiently lay on the floor waiting to mount the only remaining delivery couch. Noticeably the women would pace around hyper-ventilating, trying to ward off the noxious labor pain. It is a body time-programmed abdominal pain which must occur repeatedly before the baby can be born. When you observe their abdominal rhythmic response you can tell that the recurrence and abatement of the pain is next to precision. For a minute or so the women would be simmering with excruciating pain. Then the pain would disappear only to regroup and come back again. At the early stages of labor the pain cycle would be set at every ten minutes. Then be reset at every five minutes and shorter thereafter, until the baby is born.

The use of any kind of analgesia to stop the pain was not only considered luxurious but out of the tune with the existing native culture. To the pregnant women, enduring labor pain was considered essential. The more intense it is, the better the pregnancy outcome. So it must not be taken away. The womanhood of anyone who couldn't take the pain was in doubt. This is only one of the many superstitious belief that enveloped the medical practice in this misery poorly overgrown African country. Exposure to labor pain was also regarded as part of a punitive measure that would deter the high level of fecundity in the face of abject poverty that existed in Burundu. That notion was also a tolerable way of medical practice. Supported by the medical professionals.

Dutifully the delivery room male orderly kept a tab on the progress of laboring women. He strolls in every now and then to remind the women of the rule they got to play by. "Keep taking deep breath. Keep holding it. Do not try to push out your baby yet. Your time shall definitely come. We only got one delivery couch available." The orderly would carry on as if the women had any control over the progress of labor and childbirth. Not infrequently the orderly would get frustrated because the women wouldn't heed to his advice. The women seldom take his instruction seriously. When he turns his back they would thumb their fleshy noses on his flat buttock. They would liken his two glutei to the shape of a pair of bathroom slippers. He knew that the women always do that. He could sense it each time he walks away from them. He tries very hard to control his temper. Often times he would lash out on the already overburden women. "How come you mothers keep coming here? When would you women be contented with so many kids in your misery lives—families of ten, twelve, triplets, quadruplets? Still you keep going. "How did the child race begin?"

Their responses over the years have been ambiguously inconsistent. They do not know why they have so many children. Perhaps they wanted the kids so that they could name them. Name them after their previously deceased child. Name the newborn to ridicule the wickedness of death. That was all they can do in their helpless mind of revenge towards a monstrous enemy as ugly as death. They characterized 'death' as if it were a person to be picked upon. Anything to keep death away from them and their children.

Burundites are so much fascinated with names. It is more like a ritual than a tradition. A baby could have more than twenty names depending on how large the extended family and surviving relatives are. From maternal great-grand mother to aunts of the baby's God-father. Everybody would send in their own name proposal once the news break that the woman has taken-in. They believe that the more names they propose the better chance the baby would beat the odd of dying. Often times they sew the names together creating a snaky long barricade name. To guard against the intrusive hand of death. Very much like doctor Oligo—'s name. The natives make so much fuss over the names that they loose sight of the mother-baby delivery room agony.

The male orderly made his round one more time to repeat himself to the labor sapped women. "Please do not have your baby until you are called upon to do so". He sounded like a recorded tape. If the women dare make their delivery precipitous, their babies would lay on the same floor mat just like the mothers. The babies would be expected to sneeze, cough and breathe their way to safety until the midwife is ready to extend a helping hand. Many babies perished as a result.

Those women destined for caesarean section enjoyed somewhat better attention. The Obstetric Surgeons abhors any sort of mismanagement that would further curtail their tendencies to operate. For one thing, there were very few women signing up for cesarean even when medical indication were clearly demonstrable. Many Burundu women shied away from this new procedure. The caesarean section takes away the pain, which is accepted as a fulfilling part of a successful childbirth. They considered c/s a shade less gratifying than a real child-birth. It is hard to imagine how much labor pain those women love to bear.

Babies let out high pitch screams after taking their first breath as the obstetricians pull them out from their mothers cut womb.

Overzealous but handicapped midwives used their lips to suction out mucus secretions from babies nostrils. If time permits they spit out the mucus on the sand through the window. If not they swallow it down their throat, trashing their stomach..

So many babies that brought so much joy. Each passing that critical task of making it through the first breath. It is a matter of life and death.

It was seventeen years ago when Oligo's mother gave birth to him in this same labor ward. Oligo was her eight surviving child and she was unafraid of what the outcome would be. She had been there ten times before. Weighing only four pounds and one ounce baby oligo sneaked out on his mother before she could get whatever available help that came from the midwife. Oligo's mother did not count on that happening. And unlike all her previous deliveries baby Oligo did not cry when he fell off the birth canal.

"Something got to be wrong with this baby" the high parity mother surmised. She did not need to be a midwife to know that. Cry equals good outcome, baby remaining silent at birth is not so good. That threw her off balance. All her preparedness abandoned her as she watched her son turn from pink to blue. Was this going to be all that she had labored for? Nine months of pregnancy. A lifeless little baby boy in her hands? "May the mystery of God descend upon my son", she prayed as she shielded her newborn from the looming sword of death.

The male orderly made the rounds just on time to save another baby from becoming part of the mounting death statistics.

"Remember the kiss of life", his voice resonated from behind the vertical window metal bars adjacent to the labor room. A convenience place through which he monitors prevailing situation.

As the wake up voice of the Orderly came, Oligo's mother lifted up a heavy heart and a saddened face. In a rare synchronization of unexplainable events, a tongue of gentle breeze blew past her. Her nose was there to inhale from it. It's aroma was livelier than a new budding rose flower. It's strength larger than the might of the biblical Samson. This breeze without any doubt was far superior than her waning stale breath. She felt a surge of creative energy and a new life within. She went down on her knees, glued her swollen lips around that of her baby's. She gave baby Oligo multiple doses of her breath. "It worked!. It worked!". What a natural magical priceless medicine. In a matter of seconds the baby's color unraveled from blue to pink. Baby Oligo came back to life with a roaring high pitch cry.

From the root of her hair Oligo's mother loosened a hair thread to tie off the long cord that had linked her in the womb with baby Oligo. She knew she had to do that quickly to prevent the baby from losing a lot of blood into the redundant placenta.

Young Oligo could not believe the circumstances surrounding his own birth. His mother had told him every little miracle that had occurred that very day. "You almost slipped away from me the very first day", the heroine mother had told her son. "I knew you were given to me for a special reason. The same day you were born five other babies let go only to fall into the bottomless pit of death". Oligo could not stop thinking about his brush with death at such an early age.

Where would he have been if the male orderly had not noticed the impending doom? What if the magical tongue of breath never came? What if her mother had not acted as courageously as she did? How would the almighty jury have judged his malleable soul? Perhaps by the sins of his forefathers. He wasn't too sure about it. Most importantly where would he have gone to if he had died? Not sure of that either. But no doubt his flesh could have fed the greedy appetite of the kingdom of termite. Crunching his infant cartilage like the omnivorous caterpillar would devour the tender stem of a young plant. This did not seem to make too much sense to him. Could God have allowed this to happen? He was only an innocent baby. But what about his cousins and siblings who did not make it beyond the delivery room? What about his uncle that was with him only sixteen hours ago? What did they do wrong? "Where are they now? Do they realize that they have died? Maybe they think they are still sleeping. Wallowing in their endless dreams of infinite possibilities. It could well possibly be that those departed souls have begun a new life somewhere on earth. In some outer space? In some other planets away from the prying eyes of the living? Perhaps gone to a tiny little obscure town where nobody can recognize them. For that long? All because they parted with their breath. It was very hard for young Oligo to completely swallow. His throat wasn't deep enough.

He was only seventeen years old at the time. The age at which his inquisitiveness reached an insatiably thirsty level. It needed to be watered. Nobody was mentally ready to irrigate the capillarity of his curiosity. Not anybody in Burundu where he grew up. The folks were mired in the mix of their regular activities. Making babies and burying the dead. Activities they considered very normal.

Situations continued to deteriorate. A new low was reached in Burundu's health care delivery system. At a time when the rest of the medical world has penetrated the fortress of the cellular nucleus, amassing tremendous equity in natures own creations, doctors in Burundu are still looking up to the herbalists to show them how to tell the poisonous mushrooms from the medicinal foxgloves. Mosquitoes continue to unleash biological extermination comparable to the human annihilation that occurred in the Nazi camps. What a shame that a boneless frail looking insect could weep the breath out of millions of Burundites. Sending them to their untimely eternal rest.

But what is it that makes life and death hinge on a simple involuntary activity such as breathing. Especially the first breath we took as we emerge from our mothers womb. Why must we inhale before we experience life? Conversely why does the final exhalation lead to death?

Over the years researchers have tried to explain the physiology behind that 'first breath'. What is it in that first breath that makes it so indispensable? Did it come directly from God? Is it individually specific like the genetic book of life, the 'DNA'? Is the 'first breath', a heavenly covenant heavier than the judgment day?

No one has ever lived who had not inhaled that first breath. No matter how much they tried, medical scientists have never been able to fully elucidate the mystery surrounding the first breath. Neither Darwin hypothesis of the human evolution nor the big bang theory of human existence ventured to go head on head with this medical puzzle. It has been a fight left to be fought another day. Or even another century or millennium years to come. The teachers of the art of medicine neither knew nor understood who or where this inspirational revelation would emanate from. They couldn't even begin to conceptualize the application of decoding such a mystery. All they knew is that they have equipped each students mind with the guts to question the unknown and torment the domain of impossibilities. Setting off an avalanche of fiery intellectual pursuit that glows inside the crucibles of generation of students. Anyone of the medical students could prove to be a product of intellectual wizardry and untwist the hidden mystery inherent in human breath.

Events after events, calamities after calamities continue to prod humanity. To challenge the norms. To seize the bull by the horn and ride to the next level of human existence where mankind can no longer expire and be discarded. Where our bones could no longer be cremated and spread across the rivers. Why mankind has not taken the bet seriously has continued to puzzle young Oligo beyond his wits. New and old politicians alike have craftily left out this issue from their laundry lists of archaic redundant manifestoes. Every budgetary squander-mania has failed to earmark a penny for this purpose. Yet every new day brings on another demise, another deceased, another widow, another orphan, another grief, another broken heart.

The noise from the aging respirator got louder drowning all other activities taking place in the operating theater. Somehow that was good. Good for a change. Anything that would replace the memory of the hustling and bustling occurring in the delivery room, from the contagious weeping and wailing of the newborns, from maternal anguish as the baby descends from birth canal. From the endless rituals of funeral processions and ceremonies. It was a welcome development.

The surgical theater is the inner sanctuary of the hospital bastion. Every procedure was supposed to be well calculated. Every cotton swab counted and recounted. Every surgical mop towel counted and tagged. Every artificial nails discarded. Every necessary forceps provided with a backup. Every equipment tested for condition of service. Every contagious medical student ejected. Such was the seriousness years ago.

Removal of a diseased appendix is a routine operation. Considered the bread and butter of surgical procedure. Often times it can be done in less than twenty five minutes. Twenty minutes for an experienced surgeon such as doctor Zimzor. But time has changed. So were expectation.

"Alices! Geeve' me Alices". His voice was drawn and fatigued "Could someone, for goodness throw some Alices to me?" He begged again But no matter how long or how sticky the surgeon pleaded he was not going to get his favorite operating forceps. None was available. The last 'Alices' were buried months ago. Buried in the landscape of the nations political upheaval. Stratified by cycles of instability consequential to the military toppling their civilian counterparts and vise versa.

There would be no more hopes left of replenishing those two prongs artery forceps necessary to clamp bleeders during surgical operations. Eighteen months of looting the national treasures and smearing themselves all over with stolen oil has resulted in a paralyzed medical infrastructure and created a wide area of hairless alopecia at the crown top of medical ecosystem. The country's wealth and health had bled so badly that it was in a state of anemic shock. Anybody sent to any of the teaching hospitals suffering from any serious illness is sure to die. Patients rot until they give up their last breath and die. Hospital beds were turned into death beds. Hospital laboratories, cafeteria, lecture and patient rooms were abandoned to roaches and rats that roam about as worthy champs after crawling the ladder of human misguided egoistic frailty. The situation was complicated because the army boys had banned any form of gathering by the doctors, throwing them into a spell of neurotic panic and inaction.

Their vocal leaders who prescribed that multiple shots of tranquilizers be given to the country's cream-head president and his cohorts of thieves, were cast away in tuberculosis infested tombs called jail. Doctor Beko has been in jail for eleven months and counting, so were so many of doctor Oligo's professors. The more fortunate ones with vestiges abroad betrayed the cause, abandoned their dying patients and confused students to seek refuge in Europe, America and the Caribbean. Others renounced their profession and went underground. Many with no coping skills outside the constrains of hospital white coat hanged themselves using the branches of their stethoscope. A few would-be heroes stuck around to salvage what was left of the system. They removed tumors chewing on it's blood supply with their canine teeth, diagnosed diabetes by leaking patients urine and performed x-rays using the haziness of their visual acuity.

As the verbal stalemate in the theater continues the squeaky ventilator tagged along. It could quit anytime with no warning. The silence viciously fed on itself to produce yet a greater dense of more palpable silence. None of the vocal auxiliaries wanted to crack the egg-shell of silence. Everybody was hyper vigilant on what they would say, and how they would say it. Only a fool dared take side on the sharp edge of an irate surgeon. Definitely not Ms. Newman if she can help it. All eyes were set on her to see how she could handle the situation. All ears funneled towards her to hear how she was going to say whatever she had to say. Ms. Newman's fingers moved nervously to her face to begin playing with the single black mole buried in the bushes of her right eyebrow. It is her usual cheeky way of buying time before confronting any bloated situation. She picked on her mole back and forth. Each time examining the pulp of her index finger for stains. Going for the third pick she found the right words. "Sorry chief but we can not find any 'Alices' in the entire hospital". "None is available", she reinforced.

Nurse Newman knew that she has to use all her managerial skills to wriggle out of this mess. She always pray not to come to work on days like this. When stress make crack lines on everybody's long face.

The Surgeon acknowledged her apologies with yet another armor of deafening silence. What he would do next is anybody's guess. He is known to quickly walkout in the middle of an operation when he had not gotten the exact instrument of his choice. Nobody doubted his temperament to do so again.

For obvious reasons he decided not to pull that foolish walkout stunts today. The surgeon was grappling with a complicated appendicitis. A rupture with pus spill into the peritoneal cavity. He kept his cool as he suctions more pus from the patient's peritoneal cavity. Like water poured over oil flood of blood maintained a fairly separate track from the pus. The thick yellow drain dragged hesitatingly through the transparent hose to collect in a receptacle positioned on the floor. The theater floor vibrated around the location of the receptacle. Suction power was inadequately weak and flow has to be aided by heightened gravity. Another improviso that further tightened the grip around the surgeon's vocal cord. Soon a twenty minute operation turned into a two-hour duel. Still nobody was willing to completely break this jinx of silence. Nobody was even trying to. Only the chief surgeon has the awe-inspiring personality to elicit a belly laugh and diaphragmatic sob from the rest of the operating team. So far his fun receptors were switched off. There was too much anger in his throat suffocating the words as they migrate down from his cerebrum. However he was finding it extremely difficult to ignore one person, the fourteen-year-old girl under the blade of his knife. She was beginning to move her toes at each cut and pull. The surgeon wanted to move faster to avoid using excessive anesthesia. But his speed was crippled without his preferred operating instruments.

Using the tips of his fingers the surgeon teased out more visceral tissue before clamping the base of the appendix. Tied and cut off the inflamed distal end. Made a surgical purse string into which he buried the remaining appendicular stump. He has done thousands of this before. It was a routine standard procedure for him.

By now the patient has began swatting her hands across in an attempt to localize the direction of the noxious surgical pain. She couldn't bear it anymore. But her hands were partially restrained to the side as she lay across the full length of the operating table. It would have been inexcusably inhumane for the surgeon to continue with the operation. He abruptly stopped to do a secondary survey of the operation field.

The sick girl lay covered from head to toe under drabbed sheet of surgical gown. A distorted circular slit exposed the external landmark of the appendix at the lower right hand of the abdomen. The outside daylight provided the only illumination guiding the surgeon's blood shot eyes. The over-hanging fluorescent bulb has been dead for weeks. The army captain turned minister of health had been contacted to at least provide funds for light bulb replacement. He fired back with a brisk response. "No funds, use sunlight"

"Where is the anesthetist? Patient is waking up", the surgeon screamed? Meaning, patient is feeling too much pain. "Here I am" the anesthetist answered, cracking his neck to the left and to the right. He was half hidden behind the ventilator. His other half covered by the excesses from the patient's long surgical cover sheet. You can tell by the tone of his voice that he was drifting away into another catnap. Judging by the ease with which this particular Anesthetist always follow his patients to sleep, he either suffers from narcolepsy—irresistible urge to sleep or indulges from gas leaks coming from the old squeaky ventilator. Today, like everybody else he had to try to stay awake. The boss's itch is everybody's eczema. And everybody is scratching and uncomfortable. The anesthetist recovered quickly to deliver more sedating halothane gas. "Continue chief" he growled to the surgeon, "patient is asleep".

The surgeon eased out a short sigh of relief, rubbed his left ear with a shrugging movement of his shoulder and began to thread black suture through the eye of the straight needle. He then applied ten stitches using the mattress technique to close up the patient's skin. When he was done he turned to his young medical student and looked him over.

Doctor Oligo was still in his aseptic observatory posture. It was his first day as an assistant in the theater. He made sure he dressed up impeccably to the last detail. Upper half of his body dressed in layers of inner white shirt, outer green scrub, an ashy overall gown, a facial mask and a head cap. His lower body clothed in green scrub- pant and an elastic boot cover that ended just above both ankles. Two latex gloved hands locked snugly together and resting prayerfully at the level of his xyphisternum, the dip where the chest meets the abdomen.

"Bring your hands here" the chief surgeon said to him. Obediently, doctor Oligo surrendered his two hands into that of doctor Zimzor's. He laid doctor Oligo by his two hands and dunk them in a pool of blood which had accumulated in-between the patient's cover sheet. "This, doctor", he declared almost jokingly looking at the young medical student's blood dripping hand "is the evidence that you were an active participant in this appendectomy". The young medical student was too intimidated to react. He knew he had not assisted in any form or shape. He wouldn't be a surgeon anyway so he thought. They use their hands more than their brain.

The only air-conditioner in the theater was spitting out fire mixed with debris instead of cold air. A female aid was positioned to blow some air across the chief surgeons sweaty face with a thin wooden board. Her feminine aura employed to mellow the surgeon's fury. Doctor Oligo could feel a rivulet of sweat trickle down from his armpits down to his flanks. However his external combustion was nothing comparable to his internal distress.

Finally the patient was on her way to the dingy recovery room. The transporter aloof and demoralized. Pushing and lifting the bed that carried the post-op patient. The rusty wheeled bed refused to roll freely. The tug was energy sapping for the frail borderline malnourished transporter. He only made it midway to the destination.

Then the unthinkable happened. The young girl began to gasp for breath. She was rushed back to the operating theater. The main players were getting ready to leave. But their presence wouldn't make a difference. The anesthetist had been jolted from his slumber.

He began dishing out the orders. "Airway, Oxygen, breath, air, respiration. Common, could someone bring a fresh oxygen cylinder here? Right now. This patient is about to die. She is air hungry. That is what this patient needs to live. Can someone hear me?" He was shouting on top of his voice

"We ran out. We used up the last molecule of oxygen". The theater attendant was very candid and forthcoming in his explanations. "No more oxygen remaining in the cylinder", he said again. He tossed up the cylinder to demonstrate it. The cylinder flew up in the air lighter than a helium filled balloon. He opened the nozzle to prove it beyond any reasonable doubt. The oxygen tank made a weak yawn of final exhaustion.

"What do you guys want me to do?" The Anesthetist inquired from the rest of the disabled team. Nothing, as a matter of fact. Too late. The patient died as she let out the remainder of her last breath

Forever the 'last breath' and death will continue to mystify mankind. Even more mysterious than birth and the 'first breath'.

Doctor Oligo's mind was roasting with tension and inner turmoil. To him there would never be an end to the long hours of torture. He was a prisoner held hostage by the restlessness of his own mind. Crunched between the crossfire of his thought and the unfolding drama in the theater.

If only there was a way to make people free from sickness. Or more importantly bring them back to life after they have died. A physical reborn which restores the cells of every organ and brings them back to perfection. Free from all time precipitated malfunctions and environmental insult. So that once and for all mankind does not have to worry about dying from sickness. This would be much more fruitful than standing still like a mummified corpse watching a three-hour operation. With nothing to show for it. No matter how hard you try patients die anyway.

How he wished he could learn to change all that. That his professors can include that in the medical curriculum. Replace postmortem medical autopsy lectures with that of intra-mortem medical resurrection. Fill up that gaping hole in the quest for cure. At least make an effort to introduce the subject to them. Of how to awaken the intellectual gigantism in a students mind. That would enable the students to not only heal the sick but raise the dead. When would the department stop limiting the students to primitive echolalia and memorization of countless obscure medical syndromes. He deplored the idea that the only way to teach young medical students is as if they were apprentices learning a new carpentry skill. If he had anticipated that he wouldn't have gone to medical school. He would have stayed home to learn vocational trade from his grandfather who is handier than a goldsmith.

More surge of adrenaline gave legs to his thoughts and rewarded his imagination with twinkles in his eyes. Scores of goose pimples emerged on the skin of his torso elongating his pride. "Yes" he bragged internally "the last breath", almost whispering between his tight lips, "I have stumbled into something extraordinarily big". He looked around to see if anybody had witnessed his excitement. Nobody was paying attention. Good! In no time he could be walking down the graveyards. Knocking on all those tombs to wake up their occupants with a jolt of 'inspigorate'.

But mere tugging on the confines of the death casket generated more questions than solutions for doctor Oligo. "If life begins with a simple first breath at birth and ends with a tenuous last breath at death, certainly it would be reasonable to reconnect life by restoring that which has been lost. If indeed life is given when one breath is taken and expires when the other breath is forsaken, it wouldn't be far fetched to conclude that somewhere between the two breath lies the answer to the puzzle of reversing human demise.

Are these two breath part of a spectrum that connects the sustenance of life, from one nanosecond to another nanosecond, from one generation to another generation? Is death so intimidating that mankind is ignoring a weapon so logically simple? Is this all there is to life and death, or does life reside isolatedly in the twists and turns of the DNA helix? Was the creator giving mankind a lead when he employed the powers of breath to put life into a sculptured man?

Genesis chapter 1,verse 7, reads as follows. "Then the Lord God took some soil from the ground and formed a man out of it. He *breathed life giving breath* into his nostril and the man begin to live". If God did that to a mere formless soil, can mankind repeat that feat to a man deprived of his breathe. A dead man? Perhaps it is not impossible. To garner enough craftsmanship to be able to reconnect that 'last breath'. That last breath that when it exits makes man nothing but a mere load of ash.

Why not? Man does have the capability of doing the unthinkable. His achievements has eclipsed the wildest of all imagination. Look at the product of the 'Wright brothers' perseverance. Man has conquered the pull of gravity. Landed himself to walk on the moon. Plucked out atoms from impervious metals. Harvested their electrons and protons. Some communicate freely with the dead. If man could develop the awareness to see well into the future. Then there are no boundaries to what powers he can posses or to what skills he can learn. Reversing death included.

What if someone was gifted enough to invent a device called 'inspigorate' to harness the energy of that first God-given breath, or that of the last breath or the series of nascent breath we take everyday before they become diluted by the mix of man-made atmospheric impurities. A device that would launch that elusive breath in its most natural form to permeate across the cell wall through the cytoplasm to the nucleus. A device that can restore the cellular electrochemical balance. The sodium, the calcium and the potassium gradient. Thereby invigorating the electrical brilliance of the cell and its powerhouse, the mitochondria. Purging every dead cell of every organs of every system of their cancerous, aging and virulent infirmity. Awakening them on its trail. From the brain tissue to the heart and to the lungs and the kidneys and the intestines and the bones and skin.

Would it be possible by so doing to raise all the dead body tissues, restore organ functions and let the dead man walk again?

Could that be a recipe more therapeutic than any preparations produced by the pharmaceuticals? Could it? Could it dwarf the benefit of the growth hormone? Could it cut gene therapy application to size? Could it? Could 'inspigorate' make 'shock paddles' of a defibrillator look like an early man's hunting weapon?

Would it be possible to bottle up this quantum of life giving breath so that everyone could carry it around? Just like people carry 'epipen' in their pockets in readiness to save life during deadly allergic reaction. How about capsules of the most natural breath in it's purest form instead of cylinders of cumbersome oxygen tanks wrapped round wheel chairs. Is this all there is to dealt the final blow to that surreptitious mankind predator, death?" It was deja vu all over again for doctor Oligo. If this hypothesis tests out to be true, he had no choice but to be immortalized side by side with other great men like Isaac Newton, Craig Watson, Professor Odeku just to mention but a few. Yet he despises fame with all its conflicting whirlwind publicity. If his hypothesis tests out to be futile, null and void, his name would be relegated to the historical waste baskets of great 'wannabes' who in their shallow simplicity of mind thought the earth was flat not round. Or those in their forward looking foolish greed thought that heaven was a physical mansion devoid of infirmities. Either way he intends to pursue this to the very end for posterity sake.

Immediately, doctor Oligo saw himself destined for greater glory. Here he is with an inspiration [if fully consummated] could reshape the chessboard in the game of medical practice. That is what he is going to work on. Not cut and patch the human body like Surgeons do. No more countless blood drawing. No more piles of dizzying pills. No more signing those death certificates. No more clandestine calls from medical examiners. No more giving evasive answers to bereaved relatives. No more dealing with fleas of organ donor agents. No more searching for the cause of deaths. No more excuses. He will confront death with open arms knowing that he will triumph.

Physical and mental drill however is something he can not opt out from if he wanted to graduate from medical school. It is touted and preached as a prelude of how the medical pathway is going to be. A road laid with thorns, sharps, stop signs, tears, booby traps and mad glue. "You better shape up or ship out" is the slogan.

Class group 'B' where he belonged is made up of forty students. Thirty men and ten females. Ages between Seventeen and twenty-two. They represented the best the nation can offer. Selected from the cream of the academic dessert. Competition was rife since instructional materials were very limited.

Following the end of the marathon embryology lecture the Group separated from the rest of the class. The Indian embryologist covered the entire two hundred-page book in less than an hour. "It is my job to rattle" he said "and the student's job to retain".

There was hardly anytime to recover in-between lectures. One minute was all they had left to get to the next class. Stampede feet of restless students carried the activities over to the "Gross Anatomy Dissection" building.

The outer architecture of the anatomy class easily blended with the rest of the medical structures. A mighty drum stationed outside at the corner provided an appreciable degree of cold effect inside. Ironically it is the only hospital building left with functioning air conditioning unit. The inside is a coffin shaped heptagon. Lead based paint peel off the wall from all of it's seven corners. The unfinished floor makes the students stagger unsure of their professional future. Their footsteps awakening a tornado of dust underneath.

An inner smaller room is built out of the wall of the main room from the head of the heptagon. Resembling the inner pocket of a pocket. The smaller room is separated from the main room by a mid centered wooden counter and two flappable doors above and below it. As the medical students crowded in through the only narrow entrance door the attendant began wheeling cadavers on to the dissecting tables. "Four students to each cadaver", he reminded them. For your information, he continued "there will be no gloves provided today". "Boo, boo", was all that came from lips of some of the enlightened students. "Take it or leave it" the attendant fired back. Soon bodies of all sexes and sizes will lay on the tables. Striped of all personal identification and dignity.

Mindless of what diseases their prey died from, the students would pounce on the bodies like greedy butterflies in dire hunger for nectar. Often hopping from one body to the other looking for lean easy to dissect cadavers. They would be searching, probing, tugging, nipping, digging for arteries, veins, nerves and all what naught with their bare hands. Peeling away multiple layers of body tissue. Beginning with the skin, down to the adipose tissue until they hit the bone. Senior students who have mastered the art of cut and tear take delight in showing off to their junior colleagues.

It was December 9, 1972. The room seemed busier as students running for political post came in to use the forum to ratchet in support. "Cast your vote for me" one said "I will make sure you are supplied with more and better cadavers. If you vote for me", he continued "you will be building your future on the rocky petrous part of the temporal bone" It was intriguing for doctor Oligo to hear senior medical students talk with such ease about a complex subject. Down the line he had no choice but to master how to unearth even the most unimportant tissue in the body. Tracing every muscle, from their origin to their point of insertion. From the trapezius muscle at the back to the sartorial muscle in the thigh. Identifying all the geometric impressions built in by the creator. From the angle of Luis in the chest to the femoral triangle in the groin.

Two female students casualties were carried away on the first day. They collapsed in freight on recognizing a mutual friend among the cadavers. They were excused, only to come back the next day to make up for the lost session after the body had been removed.

Every now and then doctor Oligo would go into seclusion pondering what kind of system would desecrate the dead by throwing out their bodies to be teased and cut by a bunch of stone hearted medical apprentices in the name of medical education. What if down the road of possibilities he unravels how to restore the last breath? When every dead man and woman would be woken to walk the face of the earth again. Would these molested dead be walking again in their skeleton? Which is all they are left with after the academic insult.

By the fall of the year 1976 two hundred mint Doctors were ready to be turned loose on the nation. It was a record number coming from a premier teaching hospital in Burundu. Lots of jubilation. Finally more soldiers would be unleashed to fight against the threat of mosquitoes, tsetse flies, house flies and the diseases they carry.

A modified Hippocratic oath was faithfully administered. Doctor Oligo never really got to memorize the pledge and had to hum and mime along with the rest of his classmates. "Above all do no harm" was the only phrase that echoed repeatedly in his mind. It was indeed an event to cherish. The class was lined in five rows starting with the height disadvantaged colleagues to the more physically endowed Doctors. He was sandwiched in the middle of the second row. Only his heavily bearded face and morbid facial frown made him locatable to his cousin for a photo snap shot during the swearing in ceremony.

Before the awards were given out, the dean of medicine gave a brief speech. "Do not assume that the system has prepared all of you for greatness. If we were to follow the natural tendency of events, among the two hundred of you graduating today, some, repeat, some will whittle down by the wayside. Not knowing exactly what they want to do or where they would be going from here. Their names would be forgotten by the treacherous system in which you will soon find yourself. Yet another few of you will swiftly excel. These geniuses among you shall be the captains in their chosen field of medical pursuit. They hardly would have second thoughts in their goals and aspiration. Their names will be highlighted in annals of medical journals. They would be the future 'Charles Darwin, Jonas salk, Salako etc. The majority of you I must say will just be average. They will learn how to put band aides on multiple human infirmities. They will eventually get married, have children, get old and get over with the rest of their live span. Which, by the way, is fifty for males and fifty two for females".

Few names of outstanding students were called to receive special awards. Nothing surprising. The familiar bookworms, and the 'future-high-hopes' that distinguished themselves in the field of anatomy. Oligo did not quite make it to that coveted dean's list. He had been robbed a distinction and his name de-lineated from the deans list for arguing with the external examiner. While Doctor Oligo maintained and refused to back down on his hypothesis that death may be reversed by infusing the body with an energized quantum of nascent breath the external examiner dubbed him a young over-vibrant thinker who dared to run where the arch angels failed to thread.

The class of 1976 turned out to be the most itinerary class in the sixty year of the medical school existence. Not long after graduation all but a handful of his classmates left Burundu to Europe and America. Stepping in the shoes of their teachers who continue to flee one after another. A calamitous brain drain was ravaging the intellectual resources of the nation. Anybody who knew where to obtain a passport and a visa left Burundu. From the elementary school teachers through the engineers to the businessmen. Thousands of people were leaving. Forced to enrich the same imperialists who emasculated and suffocated his country's budding economy three hundred years ago.

His high school history was hardly lost on him. He had been saddened by how the Europeans flooded the shores of motherland Africa in search of wealth and prosperity. Found it in an unusual place. The soul, the flesh and the liberty of his fore fathers. Whom they rounded up and burnt as their wrists lay behind their back, bound in rusty syphilitic chains. Separating men from women. Cutting off daughters from their fathers. Sailing mothers and sons to slavery in far away new world. Where they knew no friends, have no families, have no future. Using the perspiration that trickle down their eyebrows to mold the bricks and bridges of their cities. Using the anger in their fist to plough and tame the wildest of their plantation. Castrating their men so that they bear no offspring. Using their rifles to rip open their gall. Raping their women and creating a whole generation of orphans and parentless children. Refusing to give freedom to three generation of human race.

Exterminating their lineage when they inevitably lost grip on the battle of human subjugation.

Doctor Oligo had vowed to remain in Burundu to make a difference. Never would he set his foot in a land with such a devious oppressive past. Never. Besides, there are many things a progressive young doctor could lay hands on in the community. Infant mortality is on the record rise. Premature babies are left to the mercy of their last breath. Mosquito has remained the only persistent plague inflicted to man. Starvation, malnutrition, health ignorance, superstitious beliefs are on the rise. Tetanus secondary to scarification marks surges ahead. Abominable children's immunization failure, horrific maternal deaths, surgical blunders, kwashiorkor, female circumcision, marital bondage, child abuses. Name it, it is on the rise. Preventable blindness. Plummeting life expectancy. There was more than enough problems to occupy a young doctor.

With the unsolicited help from his great paternal Uncle he was able to set up a village based medical practice. Great Uncle Eddy did not want the young doctor to have any excuse to flee Burundu. After all, he was the family pride. He was the first doctor in his village. A lot of folk were counting on him to be miraculous in stopping the carnage of death. So Uncle Eddy made sure he provided doctor Oligo with all he needed to start off a medical practice. Soon patients began to troop in. His practice began to blossom. His reputation began to spread like wildfire. Scores of indigent, sick children would line up with their parents to consult him on their never-ending diseases.

He succeeded in creating an aura of supernatural touch about his expertise. So he was elevated in the mind of his patients and the villagers. Anybody he laid hands on would recover from his or her afflictions. Finally they have found a messiah to take away the scourge of death. Poverty stricken mothers would leave their sick children by his consultation door and wander away knowing that the milk of his good heart will flow out and soothe their pain. Never had he turned any sick away for reason of indigence. He couldn't if he tried. Everybody knew him down to his genealogy, and when they go that deep they invariably would establish a relationship with him. "Okay let them go" doctor Oligo would frequently say to his staff. "We do not have to bill them for my services. They do not have money, besides they are part of my family".

The village in which Oligo was raised began when his great grandfather arrived three generation ago. He worked the farms and was good at it. The villagers rewarded his success with three wives. Oligo's great grandmother was the last of them all. Each of the wives had plenty of children. Grown up children were a great asset in the village. They were means of keeping up with the much needed human work force. Any meaningful mechanized means of farming was unavailable. Hoes and sticks were the most sophisticated instruments available. The females among the children were committed into marriage before they experienced puberty. Thus, making sure that there is no discontinuity in the village human life/death equation. As a result what began with the entry of a single man in no time reached a growth plateau. A village of a quarter million people at the last count. With each wave of disease epidemic, the jungle of life is trimmed. Leaving only the fittest to survive.

Looking back through the historical memories of those rocky years ,Oligo saw that he has better moments in front of him. All his childhood dreams are eventually coming to pass. Occasionally, he would lapse into remembrance about events that happened when he was a child. Growing up, surviving and living were a formidable challenge. Born, and raised in his little village south of the Saharan desert across the Atlantic Ocean. Ambient temperature never falls below eighty degrees of Celsius. He likened himself as a corn thrown out to the scorching heat of the desert. Many of his playmates fell pray to the devouring canine teeth of death. He beat the odds. His neighborhood was a village emerged in the fortress of tall trees and undisturbed bushes. Night was especially challenging. His mother would lay him to sleep and then prays over him, summoning not only one or two but four archangels to guard the four corners of his bed. Only the masquerades and the brave titled men dare venture out in the darkness of the night. The creaking sound of the crickets, the rampant intrusion of snakes, the occasional sighting of big cats made the night eerie and prevented the children from going outside to void in the near bush. Streetlights were non-existent. Hooded yam plants riding on long poles provided shade to the already dark and spooky nights. Moonlight was the only way of navigating narrow pathway leading to thatch roofed houses built out of mud. When it rained water will trickle down the thatched roofs to wet his forehead. An experience that has remained indelible in his mind. Children played only against the reflection of moonlight and under the watchful eyes of their fathers. Dusk is estimated from the diminishing size of personal shadows. Dawn by the cockcrows.

For three years Burundu was engulfed in civil war. The 'Biafran' civil war, as it was known ,added horrors to the pervading nightmare. His mother tying two younger siblings on her back would clutch little Oligo by her fingers like a hawk as she ran to take cover in the thickest of the bushes. Chickens cognizant of the impending danger would also head to the closest pen to take cover. Fleets of enemy planes would drop tons of bombs on innocent civilians killing, maiming and destroying any living and none living thing on their trail. When the attack was over, the elders would crawl out of their hideouts and retrieve their dead for burial. The manner in which the older folks buried the dead, the hopelessness in their eyes, and the trembling of their voice impressed upon him that they had accepted the torture of death only for lack of any available medical intervention. It had become a part of living.

But that was thirty eight years ago. Well before doctor Oligo made it into the medical school. When he looked at the deceased, he could tell that something had been snuffed out from them. Their breath was gone. At age two or three he began romanticizing with the idea of acquiring the supernatural knowledge that would enable him to bring dead people back to life. To reconnect that last breath. If only he can trap that breath of life. Harness it before it dissipates into the atmosphere. Transform it into another kind of energy that can be stored and reconverted. Then, he would be able to go round and knock at every grave and awaken the dead.

The devils advocate in him wouldn't let the matter rest. "What if the flesh is already rotten?", It asked. "How would you reunite the spirit with the flesh? Well, he reasoned, he may not be able to help every dead man out there. If he is able to help one out of every three or four or five dead men, he will still be satisfied. That would be good for a start. As for the 'spirit', it is nothing but a pumping heart and a responsive brain. Many more times he would be troubled by that dogging question. It was becoming more of an urge. A call for action, to do it. Try it out. Say it out loud. Let the world know what he was thinking. Perhaps somebody, somewhere, somehow knows exactly what to do. He didn't want to die with this idea still enclosed in the confines of his head.

But where the heck did this inspiration come from? Doctor Oligo couldn't quite lay hand on the source of his inspiration. Some of it probably arrived from somewhere in the vicinity of his head. Others burble out from his gut feeling. Midway the thought waves seem to interfere coherently inside a weightless floating pot from which radiates a steam of conscious ideas.

Could he really grow up to harness the abilities to stop the mortality of man. To prevent people from dying? Can he do that? Would he be the gifted one out of more than four billion people in the world? There wasn't anything about him that was physically superior compared to other children around him. If anything, he was a late bloomer with diminutive body frame and gentle touch. His age mates all towered over him. However, they knew that what he lacked in flesh he had made up many folds in intuition. At an age when his mates bask in the glee of afternoon rain and played soccer on the street corners, he had shown a sense of purpose. He would walk around the neighborhood healing ailing rodents, reptiles that are in danger of dying and re-uniting them with their families. Those that he found dead he would make an effort to revive. When not possible he would give them a befitting burial.

It was usual for him to hold up in his study room for hours

re-visiting the laws of physics and nature. Wondering if he would be the modern day Isaac Newton. He had improvised a prism which he mounted on his study table. His intention was to separate the colors of the pencil of light as it streams through the window. But the colors failed to show on his paper screen. He was dejected. Perhaps he missed part of the experiment. He looked up and there they were again. The two twin lizards. They always came to check on him. He could barely see up to their gray colored redundant neck skin. The reptiles retreated. On some rare times when doctor Oligo was not on his study table the Lizs had gone in to take shade under his bamboo bed. Whenever he found rice-grain size stools on his table or stool he knew they had gone in. He would find them and evict them before he settled down for more research. He spent hours on end exercising his mind. Testing its limits. Stretching it far beyond its very last boundaries. To his pleasant surprise his mind ran very far and wide. Wider than the Nile river in Egypt. More fertile than the hanging garden of Babylon. He only needed to draw from the bounties of its treasures, at no monetary cost, no taxes. Just drawing from nature's own inexhaustible resources.

2.

In his obscure village he practiced medicine with passion and enthusiasm. His expertise and patience easily surpassed any hurdle. His patients recovered. Even though payment was none to paltry he continued to exert his maximum best. He utilized local remedies to perform extraordinary cure. He Recommended cocoanut juice for children with diarrhea; Encouraged mothers not to abandon breast milks for the cow milk; Spoke out against female circumcision, teenage pregnancy and marital bondage. He was a lone voice.

Everybody wanted doctor Oligo to see their sick loved ones. They would drop off staple crops as a show of their appreciation for all his care. The children and the parents loved him far and beyond.

He was energetic and thoughtful. His diagnosis and opinion were never in doubt. For his clients were both subservient and ignorant. He would be in at his practice at seven in the morning. Then grab whatever staple snacks the villagers had to offer him at lunch time, and then return to more work. Later he would heads home at about ten o'clock every night. On his way home he would tune on his radio to listen to some mild rock music. The lyrics, the pace, the huskiness, provided him with the inspirational motivation to carry on stronger at each passing day. Reaching home he would toss his clothes on the nearest sofa, make dinner, eat, and crash exhaustively to sleep. He needed every bit of extra rest he could get. It was a pretty much set routine for him. For a moment he knew everything was going to pass. Somehow all his dreams were coming true.

But does he have this skills yet or not? The knowledge to give life to those that have died? The abilities for which he craved so much. He was not quite sure. He has not even invented anything that looks like 'inspigorate'. Yet he yawned for the opportunity to demonstrate it. The thought of wanting to do this apparent impossibility sent a cold shiver down his spine.

Many more months had gone by and everything seemed good and dandy. Whatever he laid hands on rolled smoothly to the last dial. It seemed as though he had no more blessings left to ask. His confidence became so bloated that he increased the time he spent enjoying rock and roll music. He was quick to remind anybody who questioned his professional commitment that this kind of music spurred up his imagination and re-enkindles his resolve to continue with all the life struggles. Each time he had come up with the right answer. He was a winner of amazing talent.

Everything continued to work for him until this very day. With hardly any prior notice, the mild undulating flow of tide turned on him. Suddenly strings of bad omen had conspired to throw pebble on his wining ways. First, he woke up hurting. He had stepped on the fangs of a pregnant scorpion. The arachnid had hidden beneath his shoes waiting for him to wake up. Attacked his left pinkie toe, which was swollen and throbbing with pain. He braved it to the bathroom, into his pants, into a pair of loose slippers and off to work. He managed to infiltrate his pinky with a dose of numbing lidocaine. The shot didn't seem to help. He endured tremendous hurt all day as he limped from one sick patient to another.

How such an incident can befall a man who has been doing such a sacrificial job for his fellow men was incomprehensible to him. Doesn't heaven know that he needed every bit of his foot to move around in order to attend to his patients? Doesn't heaven understand that this is a special kind of work?, helping soothe the pains of orphans, indigents and the medically ostracized.

It was only the beginning. Nobody born of man was going to be immune from the ever-changing wave of life. Which washes ashore all that is good and bad. For now doctor Oligo knew things weren't going his way. Not nearly as favorable as it used to be. The extra energy he spent dragging his foot around left him fatigued. Yet he remained unfazed. He returned back home from work at his usual 10 pm, made his usual dinner of fried plantain over rice with fish soup. Served himself on top of his bar counter, using the long bar chair to stretch out his aching foot. In a show of religious disobedience he avoided his usual nighttime meditation. Slept awkwardly, letting his sore foot hang out from the corner of the bed. The only thing worth doing when he was woken up by a loud thundering noise was to look at the time. Two in the morning? That means he had only gotten three hours nightcap. The thundering sound of the motor bike had fouled the sacredness of the village night. The crickets had suddenly stopped creaking. The big cats temporarily sent crouching. The breezy wind seized momentarily to lend their ears to an uninvited climate intruder. Too stricken with fear the villagers refused to peer through the window. As the noise got louder, doctor Oligo knew it was coming his way. But what could have happened?, he wondered. He tied up all the loopholes before he left his medical office in the evening. None of the patients looked critically sick. The cases were unusually easy and monotonous. Victims of malaria, malnutrition and hunger. He administered as much anti-malaria shots, as needed; Gave out as much bread, milk, and personal money as he could afford, and headed home. Unexpectedly, in his gloat of another successful day, the surreptitious boomerang of Murphy's law had undercut him.

Doctor Oligo got off his bed, stepped into his pajamas and grudgingly dragged his aggravated left foot forward. He recognized the visitor and opened the front door before the visitor could bang on it.

Eppo, the office messenger is a hunk of a man. His knock is louder than thunder clap. There isn't any other person in the entire world that looked like him. At least not in the entire village. A rare mutant gene must have sowed him inside his mother's womb. At full stretch he measured in excess of eight feet. The Load of thick skin on his back and neck weighed his upper body portion down forcing him to walk around with a stoop. The rest of his body parts are carved out from iron ore. His raised hand fell back into place as doctor Oligo beat him to the punch. He raised it again to deliver the nurse's note to doctor Oligo.

The note was brief and naked "Come quickly doctor I think Judd has died in his sleep". The bad news floated for a while until it sank on him. For a brief moment you can hear the sound of a pin drop. The intervening long stretch pause was filled by the selfish sound of tickling idle seconds. In Unison the night darkness blinked further into pitch-black. Doctor Oligo's mouth was agar in astonishment. Why was he left alone to feel the pinch of this agony? How come the clock still tick away. Totally oblivious of the catastrophe. His brain wave rippled back and forth trying to make a sense out of the cosmic events. It was his first professional casualty since he graduated from medical school.

Fifteen minutes later doctor Oligo arrived at his medical facility. The lamp that lit the patient's room was beginning to sputter. The gasoline had burned through-out the night and needed to be topped. He waited.

A bunch of mosquitoes hovered menacingly around him, singing angrily with their wings. He resisted the urge to chase after them. One of them fearlessly settled on his right arm to begin siphoning blood from his tensed veins. Doctor Oligo made a muscle but that didn't scare the mosquito. It fed freely on him for twenty seconds.

Empathizing for the dead and bereaved was something nobody taught him in medical school. Emotions spill out differently depending on who the dead is. Less bearable if you are dealing with the loss of one's relative. If anything, his romance with cadavers while in medical school had made his feelings mute to dead bodies. But this incident was happening in a different arena. In his own village where he is most revered. Striped of all the protective wall of medical school. His reputation was on the line. As he stood lost on his next move, an aide handed him a stethoscope. For a doctor who dined with dead bodies during his hay days in medical school, he approached this particular corpse with great trepidation. Judd's dead body felt cold and stiff. No breathing movement of the chest. Heart beat gone. Both Pupils dilated and fixed. Finally the reality hit the bottom like a humongous stone cast in the deep blue sea. Tears of frustration filled his eyes and spilled over to the corners of his mouth. It tasted sour and concentrated.

"What in heaven's sake went wrong? He must have been dead for an hour or two". Doctor Oligo picked up the deceased chart and reviewed his management. A sixty-year-old man admitted less than eighteen hours ago. The patient never did any self destructive stuffs like cigarette smoking. He was however obese and moderately hypertensive. Nevertheless he was stable and in good spirit when he went to bed. Received his regular dose of medications before going to bed. He might have had a fatal heart attack. Now what to do? Ever since he left medical school he has never bothered expounding on how to garner the wisdom to give life to the dead. He had not harnessed that tremendous energy of the breath he dreamed of. Maybe it was just a fad after all.

What if he already posses the competency tucked away somewhere in the recesses of his persona? Well, today would be the day to test it. To show if he can do what no man has done since Christ died—wake a dead man. Doctor Oligo tried drawing a metaphysical energy to the deceased by mere focused concentration, but nothing happened. Hey!—he reminded himself, that is not what inspigorate is all about. He bent over positioning his mouth just above the patient's nose. He blew in a dose of expired air. Yes! Very close, but not quite how he imagined inspigorate to operate. But that did not work either. His breath was stench from the fish meal he had last dinner. The air impotent from adulteration. The dead laid still. He repeated another maneuver using the pouch of his palm to trap some air, which he diverted to the face of the deceased. But his palm was porous, besides, he was drawing from the pool of environmental dilution.

Predictably nothing happened. After the second futile attempt the staff nurse began staring at him wondering what the heck he was up to. "Don't worry I am okay", he said in answer to the nurse's telepathic question.

Bad events indeed have an uncanny way of happening in succession. Like a priced boxer it steps up to finish you while you are reeling from a hard punch. Doctor Oligo had not quite gotten over his recent professional loss when he was hit with more bad news.

Even though Neb did not die in his care the loss was equally as devastating. News on Neb's demise reached him in the noontime. It was the last thing he had expected. He was not ill. There wasn't anything indicating that his final hours were imminent. Up until this day the family has not accepted his eternal departure. They still wait for the day when he will ring that front door bell, step in boisterously to finally apologize for pulling a fast one on them. "Big shame on big Neb, I fooled all of you," he would say before bursting into mischievous laughter. Unfortunately, that day may never come. The loss brought doctor Oligo's medical Achilles down to its knee.

The funeral procession continued tortuously over five miles through a link of corroded suburban roads riddled with potholes. The simmering sun reluctantly gave in to a pestering drizzle. Brown dust was rising furiously to stick in the throat, thus making swallowing really arduous.

When the convoy of cars, bicycle and pedestrians reached their destination the stage was all set. The professional mourners were already weeping. The masquerades were entertaining. The widow of the deceased mourned from a tent located at a visual strategic corner. The tautness of her forehead overcome by grief. Her eyelid engorged heavily with tears. "Mum your face looks like that of a Japanese" her four year old son noted. Her hair shaved to her skull. A humiliating relic of traditional garbage. She was only in her thirties. Barely married for six years

People lined up to view the deceased. He was laid in 'state'. They walked round the bed perimetrically from the foot towards the head and back. Some stopping to pray for eternal life. Others stop to cry. While others stop to reflect on their own impending inevitable mortality. On about the ninth rotation doctor Oligo decided to join the queue.

He had known the dead man Neb for almost seven years. He was more than a brother in-law to him. They got along so well. Neb's extroversion fitted quite well with doctor Oligo's pensive personality. His handsomeness withstood the filth of death. A fixed grin gave him a false sense of well being. He was dressed up in his favorite yellow tuxedo suit. A black leather shoe decorated his feet. The shoe strings securely tied and tucked in as he would have it done himself.

Doctor Oligo contemplated on what he would do next. What role would he play right now? For God's sake this is a gathering of family members and close friends. They all knew him well for him to hide. He could hear them talking about him. It was loud and clear. Disappointed or may be even disgusted that he could not rescue brother Neb from the fangs of death. Of what use is his seven years in medical school?

By mere spontaneous body automatism he turned and looked back. Goodness he was right. They were indeed pointing fingers at him. Sweat began to rain down from his temple to merge with his tears. He stood glued to the foot of the deceased bed for what seemed to be like eternity. Once again he began to make a mental picture of concentrated energy flowing inside the windpipe of the deceased. It didn't seem to be working. He couldn't even get a strand of hair to move. Frustrated he gazed onto heaven to intervene on his behalf and rescue his medical pride. It fail on deaf ears. Humbled once more, he retreated backward to be swallowed by the teaming crowd of mourners.

As the body was being lowered to the grave, the parish priest read a few passages from the scriptures. "Thou are ash, and to ash thou shall return". The eternal departure of Neb left doctor Oligo anguished in search of direction. Of what use is he if he can not perform in situations like this? If priests are given the powers to forgive sins, unbound shackled souls and save them from eternal fire. If great historians can re-write history and make it right. Why can't great physicians be given the gift to restore physical life after death. He has had it. Nothing is guaranteed in this profession. By his own lofty standard he had fallen short. He needed to get out of town, to a place that could give credence to his ultimate goals.

But where is that going to be? Where would he have the opportunity to follow the dreams of his mind? The erstwhile great Roman Empire makes splash only in the documentary of archeological discoveries. He never really believed in England. The sun seemed to have difficulties locating the region. United States of America was the only fair alternative. The only remaining superpower amidst scores of paper tigers. However he needed to do a lot of rational deliberation before he could reconcile his goals with Americas oppressive past. A land where there are no boundaries to human dream and no obstacles to human endeavor. A land where there is no idea so esoteric to be crystallized; where the audience is so generous they would lend ears to every imagination; where people are so benevolent they would give their life savings to a cause close to their heart. Where billions of dollars are set on fire each year through the nuzzle of a spaceship. Where people are so lavish they would play fight with food in a world with one third of it's population dying from starvation. A land that has prospered and ballooned from the heap of intellectual migration. An offspring conceived out of the world collective manhood.

A family meeting was soon rallied to try to dissuade young Oligo from leaving Burundu. Seated were oligo's parents, uncles Eddy ,charley and Oligo himself.

Oligo's father began with a stern voice. "Son", he said "there would be no debate about it, you are going to continue with your practice in Burundu. I do not want to hear any more mention of you going to America".

Uncle charley sunk his two hands in a bow of water and washed off his hands on doctor Oligo's mission. Wherever your father stand on this issue, that is where I stand he said summarily. Oligo's mother took a contrary view. "Going back since my child was born, I knew he was destined for something great. Did any of you saw his flame of life withstood the extinguishing wickedness of death. He is a destined child" she repeated. "If he wants to go to America, let him go. But not before you get married" she admonished pointing her fingers directly on doctor Oligo.

On February 22 of the year 1981 he packed his bag and headed to the airport to board a 727 Boeing plane en-route to the New World. Patients and their families gathered in his office to discuss what the impact of his departure would have on the village health. 'Do not worry so much' said Mr. Eppo the messenger, 'doctor Oligo had found a replacement for the practice. His name is doctor Haggler. He is a good person and he sure knows the job'. Some of the villagers were appeased but deep in their heart they know that no other person can match the excellent practice of doctor Oligo.

'Ladies and Gentlemen in case there is an emergency, the oxygen mask will drop spontaneously over your head'—, it was the singing voice of the airhostess. The airplane taxied for the next seven minutes on the bumpy tarmac before taking off on a twelve-hour trip to New York City.

On board the plane doctor Oligo spent his time reminiscing on the limitation of his practice in Burundu. Was it his fault that a patient died in his sleep? Could it have made a difference if his facility was equipped with all the bells and whistles of the modern technology? When would the rudimentary medical practice seize to exist in the nation of Burundu?

He cannot wait to get started all over again. His in-patience was running amok. A practice in New York would be refreshingly reassuring. Probably mechanized to the teeth. A city where a robot can be made to ask and obtain information from patients while fleets of imaging machines will examine their body better than a doctor's violating cold hand. Then the robot returns to read off the diagnosis and write the prescription. All done efficiently and expeditiously. Trimming cost to the barest minimum. Devoid of human error and subjectivity

Yes!, and that is only the tip of the iceberg in the magnitude of medical evolution in front of him. Once he set foot in America he vowed to pursue his dreams to a conclusion. He would work harder than ever to reach that goal. Not for fame, but to put back smile on the face of the bereaved. To make that lad run to his dad again and be picked up and tossed in the air. To put a smile on the face of that widow once more. To let that young girl whisper secrets into the ears of her dad one more time.

He only needed some old smart colleague to lead him. It would be a beginning in the right direction. Enough of memorizing medical syndromes just for the sake of self-aggrandizement. The patients die anyway. He needed to be able to bring them back to life when they die. That to him was the finish point of an accomplished doctor. He needed the omniscient hand of the emerging computer technology to show him the way. Teach him the miracles of medical cure not the art of medical evasion. To let mankind have a second chance on life.

At thirty seven thousand feet above sea level the plane has escaped the force of gravity and cruising well above the cloud, which looked deceptively solid. Luring doctor Oligo unsuccessfully to jump overboard to walk on its airy substance. How his heart yawned to rest on it's pillows. Mountains of cloud leaned graciously on one another. Indeed it was his first time of flying that high. Of appreciating how beautiful the nature is above in contrast to the earthly chaos underneath.

Another interruption came from the crews. The trip has gone so smooth and fast. "Please have your seat belt fasten as we begin to descend to 'JFK' international airport".

It was in the middle of the winter storm. Amorphous snow rained down from the sky. Temperature was a mere 3 degrees and the wind was blowing chills. Doctor Oligo's light jacket was no match to the tormenting old man winter. He paced up and down the sidewalk looking-out for his escort who was late in arriving. His fingers and ears unfamiliar with the cold hardened into a rock. He approached a nearby white lady to ask for the location of a pay-phone. She moved away from him. He regrouped, approached a black man hauling a cart over-loaded with baggage. "Where is the pay phone around here?"—doctor Oligo asked him. But the guy wasn't sure he understood what doctor Oligo was asking. He pushed on his cart. He can not be bothered anyway with someone learning how to communicate in American phonetics. Is this a prelude of more problems to come? Hope not. Oligo assured himself.

Settling down into the city was rougher than riding a raged bull market. He soon discovered that hitchhiking into the coveted American medical system wasn't going to be easy. As he waited for the right opportunity his wallet got leaner, his face grew more wrinkles, and his hairs began to recede from the crown. The resisting hair was turned gray by the octopus hand of stress.

Many months went by and doctor Oligo grew more dysthymic of the system. Why must everything but the wheels and deals in wall street got to have a time interval. Is the system designed to be hostile to the new immigrants? A clear message that the era of Columbus type of adventurous discovery is over. Is this the America that he dreamed of? He wasn't sure anymore.

He woke up one impoverished morning to announce to his host that he must find himself a job. Any job for that matter. He was ready to work for anybody willing to pay him some money. To hell with medicine. To hell with medical resurrection. Staying alive now was all that mattered to him. He needed the money. And very fast too. He was overdue for a haircut. He was overdue for another pair of jeans. He could not keep off the gray hairs. They were coming to him like weeds to eat up the dark hairs. He urgently needed to get rid of them and level off the balding plain field.

Delivering pizza was not a job he enjoyed too well. To make it less attractive the clients managed to come up with exact change all the time. Besides, he was too medically cultured to directly ask for tips. He tried another job at a T-shirt factory. Did not last very long either. Got fired because he couldn't fold T-shirt fast enough as they cascade down the hot grill.

He knocked harder at the door of his destiny. The job hunt took him to the worlds of Manhattan. The number three train jingled him downtown to Madison square garden. He got off the train and loitered on the pavement trying to figure out his next move. He marveled at how much human traffic he had generated just within minutes of geographical indecision. Other passengers meandered around him to head to their various destination. Nobody but him looked lost. They moved faster than a programmed toy truck on a radio shack retail counter. Incredible. In no time everyone else but him seemed to have vanished. Thank goodness, eventually he sported the street sign pointing to his intended destination.

The escalator took him fast out to the naked street. It was midday. The sun had just completed it's rise. It's finger rays poking on the eyes like the pain of accidental corneal abrasion. Doctor Oligo hesitated, then took a couple of steps, shaded his eyes with the shallow curve of his left palm before gazing upward to the magnificent sky scrappers swaying in the thin air. Their intimidating magic was instantaneous. The towers dwarfed his ambition. Reducing him both physically and mentally into a tiny ranting ant hidden beneath one of their multi level basement. He felt very insignificant.

Tell me, he wondered, how in creation-time his aspiration could radiate beyond the concrete within which he has been embedded. Even when it finally escapes, can his ideas rise above the aggressiveness of those spectacular achievers. Has every real job been filled? Has every man's ideas been accomplished? Has every mans desire been met? Has every real money been made? How come the measures got to be set so high.

For two years he had no option but to bounce off from one menial job to another. The odd jobs didn't cut it. He was always broke. With each passing shirt to fold his dream kept racing away from him. He hardly remembers what he set out to do in America. Living had become more important than worrying about the dead. "Let them go in peace. Endomorphic introverts. Those are whom death strikes first. Nobody he knows is alive who is built that way".

The need to walk away from squalor pushed him to explore a residency program position at Silver Greek hospital in New York City. High time he got back on track about being a doctor. Doing the only thing he was trained to do. Enough of coming to America to be a pizza delivery man. Sick of being a newspaper vendor. He was also fed-up trying to stop criminals as a security guard with nothing but spines of folded newspapers.

3.

Doctor Oligo had waited almost two years for this day. The day he would be interviewed for a residency position. Two dreadful years of waiting to get back on track. He had grown weary of doing odd menial jobs. Jobs he did not train for. Job his messenger in Burundu would find not appetizing.

His appointment was set at 10.30 AM. Doctor Oligo rapped on the partially opened door. Entered the office when he heard Doctor Woeffry's voice telling him to come in. He remained standstill waiting for doctor Woeffry to take the lead.

Doctor Woeffry meanwhile seemed to be engrossed squeezing back his books in the crowded cabinet. He got over that hurdle only to take on another task. Without looking at Oligo's face he selected out another chunk of cookie from the crumb, threw it into his bucket of a mouth and began munching. It was a special kind of coconut cookie. He sucked on it like a diabetic on sugar crave. Again doctor Oligo waited patiently to be invited to the chair. He wanted to be as formal as the book he read had suggested.

Finally doctor Woeffry acknowledged the presence of his candidate. "Hello doctor" he said. "Good morning sir, doctor Woeffry", doctor Oligo replied over-killing the simple courtesy with a high degree of nervousness. Both men surveyed each other over. They have nothing in common.

Doctor Oligo wasn't completely ignorant about doctor Woeffry. Earlier on he had a chitchat with a classmate of his who had joined the residency program a year ago. They tried to predict which of the high ranking doctors would interview him. They reached the conclusion that that doctor Oligo had no chance in a lifetime to be interviewed by the director. Between his private practice and kissing up to management the director wastes no time with disposable medical staffs like interns. His interest lies strictly with interviewing medical billers and personal secretaries. Which leaves the odd favoring either doctor Woeffry the neurologist or doctor Bebenito the allergist. Both senior members in the department. Both respected clinicians.

Doctor Woeffry has remained one of the hottest-hidden talk about topics among residents. He is a neurologist of utmost intellect. Every other consultant checks out his diagnostic impression before they commit themselves on the patient's chart. His medical agility is never in doubt. So also is his exploitative sexual overture. According to grapevine years ago he had invited a senior resident doctor to watch a basketball game finals in his apartment. In the middle of the game doctor Woeffry made his move. He went after the resident like a cock chasing a hesitant hen for copulation. Tripping over furniture, tables, framed medical certificates, valuable make-up kits, souvenirs, long wine glasses. Nothing on his way was spared. It was only by a share act of courage and determination that the resident escaped to tell the story.

Only four feet eight inches tall his broad face inspire both awe and conquest. He propels himself around on stooped right shoulder, pair of dancing as opposed to walking feet and engorged hairs that stand stiff in single strands on his tear-drop-shape head. You can twist a ping pong ball on any one of the hairs. Large eyes separated by what stood as a mound of nasal flesh. The angle of his lips ends on the same vertical plane with the corners of his eyes.

Immediately, the men went through a series of questions and answers to determine doctor Oligo's level of professional preparedness and ambition. To Oligo's dismay the interview was very short. What a disappointment. He had spent more than two years waiting for a three minutes interview. No preambles. It was a formality. Each men had already read the others dossier.

Doctor Woeffry: "How long have you been a doctor?"

"Ten years, since 1976", doctor Oligo answered.

Doctor Woeffry: "What kind of illness did you see where you were practiced?"

Doctor Oligo: "Mainly malaria, malnutrition, diarrhea, hunger and starvation related illnesses".

Doctor Woeffry: 'What is your ultimate goal in medical practice?"

Doctor Oligo: "To be able to deal a lasting and indelible blow against man's mortality".

Doctor Woeffry: "How are you going to do that?"

Doctor Oligo: "By deploying 'inspigorate' to harness and deliver the magic powers of human breath".

Doctor Oligo: "What is 'inspigorate."

Doctor Oligo: "Let's say it is the name of the device that would carry the feat.".

Doctor Woeffry: "You are kidding?"

Doctor Oligo: "Not at all".

Doctor Woeffry: "Listen carefully doctor Oligo. I am not quite sure whether to recommend you or not, it depends on a couple of things. The department's director would be contacting you shortly. In any event if you get hired, the next three years of yours belong to us. You will be fighting the cold war. Seventy five percent of your encounter would be for the sake of common cold or of its complications. It is a no win situation. Lager than life itself. If this virus is eradicated the department would be thrown into irreparable financial harm. But as long as the virus looms, the patients keep coming and we keep making money. The resident's job keep going. The drug companies keep donating money to our cause. Everybody is happy. It is a delicate balance and no person in their mind should try to upset the trend".

"How can the viability of the entire medical apparatus be hinged on an ailment as benign as the common cold?" Doctor Oligo asked earnestly. "This wouldn't be another professional humiliation, would it?"

"Hang on for a minute I will show you" answered doctor

Woeffry. Then he propelled himself past him to completely close the front door. He returned to the outstretched hand of doctor Oligo about to say "so long". Ignored it. Instead, doctor Woeffry locked doctor Oligo in a bear hug, smooching his navel against doctor Oligo's crotch. His over silted lips wrapped around doctor Oligo's neck like a teetering vacuum. It was the quickest quikie ever. He came alright. Went through the usual transient post coital hypotonic stupor. Finally he released his grips on doctor Oligo. "Well", he mumbled, "I will put your name on the probation list for six months. If you want to retain your position after the probation is over doctor Oligo, you now know what to do".

Confounded, doctor Oligo exited the office hurriedly. Took the stairs down to the lower level where the male restroom is located. Under the reflective aid of the mirror he picked out coconut crumbs, which doctor Woeffry had injected into his mouth? He wiped his lips furiously with a tissue. It yielded thin purplish make-up. Disgusting. He spat aiming at the nearby garbage can. He missed. He hated all that. He wiped again and again with water soaked tissue until he was satisfied. He proceeded via the staircase to the main lobby to catch up with his buddy.

Fifteen minutes of eleven in the morning was rush hour time. It was a wrong time to search for anybody in the hospital main lobby. What you would see is nothing but an ocean of human traffic. Doctors returning back from grand rounds collides with patients searching for directions, crisscrossed by lovers on the look out for their dates, entangled by hooked-on coffee drinkers rushing for second refills, doted by opportunistic plain clothe cops on missions to arrest criminals who have come in for medical treatments. The scenario simulates a major electric bumper car ride.

All that doctor Oligo could do at the moment is stare at moving figures in flowing hospital white coats. He was awkwardly noticeable as he peered into black and white faces trying to make eye recognition. There weren't much individual facial dissimilarities among the crowd to guide him. Everybody looked very much like offspring of consanguinity marriages.. He wondered if human species had reached a zero cycle of physical differentiation. His perseverance soon paid off. His buddy had been displaced several meters from where he left him. Shielded by a stationary hospital security guard. Oligo's buddy had eagerly waited for more than half an hour for him to come out and tell about his encounter with doctor Woeffry.

What happened? How did it go? Did you get the Job? His buddy asked him impatiently.

"I don't know, I am not quite sure, I would rather not talk about it", doctor Oligo replied, avoiding eye to eye contact with his buddy.

A couple of days later doctor Oligo got 'the call' from the department that he got the job. It was a delightful surprise for him. This time doctor Oligo fought back tears of joy. Everybody has their moment when the sun shines on them. This could be the break that had eluded him for years. This could be the beginning of his time.

The job orientation began in full force. Three full days to go over the entire operations of the hospital. It was quite insightful.

The speaker on the first day took a brief moment to introduce himself. He ran over a couple of stairs to get to the podium. Switched on the rotating fan and took a mouth full bite out of his doughnut. "My name is Brut he said abruptly, "I am an MBA, Harvard graduate and I have been on this job for nineteen years". As he finished that sentence air current from the fan arrived to unmask the tuft of hair strands he had used to ameliorate his balding occiput. Readily he redid the strand with a four inch comb which he fished out from his breast pocket. "I am not a medical doctor he confessed but I have a doctorate in medical management". He paced up and down the stage exuding with inflammatory pomposity.

"The hospital was the brain child of a rich black mentor who wanted to ensure adequate medical care for black children during the dark ages of segregation. Since the death of the mentor twenty years ago the goals have been reversed completely. It has become that of self financial sufficiency and survival. Government has scaled down on subsidy. The hospital has been on the red before Johnny began crawling. Now Johnny is playing high school football. The hospital has whittled so down that its contemporaries are gearing to swallow it. Therefore, ladies and gentlemen always keep your eyes on the greens". And don't you ever forget this piece of advice irrespective of your background, the medical practice in this community follows the twenty eighty rule. Twenty percent is all about your knowledge and eighty percent is for your artistic exhibition.

Second day was even more scary. The interns were told to learn to do things for themselves. Do not wait for the nurses if you can triage that patient and get the line moving very fast. "Do not wait for the messenger if you can get that urine or blood specimen to the laboratory yourself. Do not wait for elevators either. Not only could you get stuck in it for hours, you would be wasting valuable time. Staircase are not only meant as fire escapes routes it can get you in and out of the laboratories. I encourage you to use them. Same goes for cleaning. You have all been told where the mops are. So, it is your responsibilities to watch out for your patients. Woe-be-tide you if any patient fall on their vomitus. You are gone. It will be the last day of your residency program in this hospital. Please do not wait for cleaners in such circumstances. You may be the only cleaner available at the time".

On the third day the Orientees have to return to the conference room for the most important introduction on medical billing and documentation. The idea they were told is to train every intern to be able to generate maximum revenue, to ward off hostile takeover of the hospital by ruthless venture capitalist. Equally important, to keep the malpractice lawyers at bay.

By 6 a.m in the morning, tens of interns have begun making their ways to the popular conference room. The connecting hallway was endless and lavishly set up. The long stretch permitted the interns to familiarize themselves with one another and exchange experiences. At the beginning of the long hallway doctor Oligo was joined by his buddy. Everybody was talkative since the three days of horror was finally coming to an end. Everybody but doctor Oligo who remained very cautiously guarded. His buddy refused to give up. He continued to squeeze on him to tell his story about the encounter with doctor Woeffry.

Evidently doctor Oligo had a lot in his mind but chose to suppress it. He wasn't going to divulge to anybody that he was forcefully kissed by a male doctor. By his up-bringing the rest of the incident is a shameful taboo of enormous proportion. He must keep it very secret.

Both friends continued to walk side by side en route to the conference room. Their feet made tip-tap sound on the glistening Italian tile that adorned the hallway floor. An intervening sheet of wall mirror captured the image of doctor Oligo's protruding abdomen. He made conscious effort to ignore it. His gaze shifted to the picture frames hanging on both sides of the parallel wall. Bursts of great alumni, brilliant inventors, accomplished researchers and generous donors stretched from top to bottom. Interspersed between the pictures were scenic views of the cloud, the sea and the galaxy. Beautifully done in natures own tempo. They seemed to have been drawn by the same anonymous artist. His name ineligible signed at the bottom of each piece.

Oligo's imagination made a trip. This is definitely one of several places where his name would end up if he can pull off this big dream of his. But he isn't sure anymore. His curiosity has faded considerably. His inspiration seemed overcome by perspiration. Which in turn vanishes into thin air. Could he be suffering from brain fatigue and rusty brain syndrome very early in the game? Only time will tell. He was engrossed in what the future holds for him.

From nowhere five pudgy fingers came to be embedded in his left buttock.

"Ouch! What in hell is going on here?" He shouted looking over his shoulders. There he was, doctor Woeffry, already sprinted far away by his pair of dancing feet. His eyes saying "play along with me or else you get booted out from this program". Finally, doctor Oligo's buddy has been treated to a life movie. What his ears could not hear his eyes have seen.

To shore up his morals and fight against the increasing

temptations doctor Oligo had begun seeing the hospital Chaplain. It was like a faith-based psychotherapy. He did not think he was quite crazy yet. Otherwise he would have seen a shrink. But again he had no time to keep any appointment with a medical specialist as rigid with time as the Psychiatrist. Not quite the same standard with the reverend. Anytime they meet, the situation not withstanding, anywhere they meet, be it on the hallway or the bathroom ,it is a therapy session.

Doctor Oligo waited long enough for the hospital Chaplain to catch up with him in the bathroom drying his wet hands.

Father Randy must have been in his early sixties. His seductive face and a permanent set of smile makes him look twenty years younger. Darting eyes matched with quick steps completed an impressive physical resume. He prefers to dress in black pants and black short sleeve shirts as opposed to the more familiar priestly robe. This makes him less reverend but a lot freer.

"Hi doctor O", the reverend greeted as always only using the first letter of doctor Oligo's jaw breaking name. "Hi reverend" he replied. The reverend went on to seize doctor Oligo's partially dried hand, stroking it back and forth between his right thumb and index finger as he talks. Doctor Oligo did not try to resist. Pulling away from the reverend's hand massage was out of the question. He wouldn't let go until you provided answers to all his double prong questions.

"How is your spiritual life? How are you coping with all the temptations in the hospital?" The reverend asked as he continued to enjoy the flesh of doctor Oligo's palm.

"What temptation?" Doctor Oligo asked attempting to answer two of the reverend's questions with one of his. He had become very defensive lately.

"I know what is going on", the reverend admitted.

"About who?" doctor Oligo asked pointedly.

"About doctor Wolf" the reverend said, purposefully mispronouncing and shortening doctor Woeffry's name.

But doctor Oligo wouldn't still confess. The reverend tactfully changed the subject.

"Did you know doctor that after death the body decays while the soul goes to be judged by God the almighty and that forgiveness, holds the key to eternal life. It would unbind your powers and exalt them far and beyond the wildest imagination of men. For that reason a man should care more about saving his soul rather than worrying about his body".

What an insightful sermon, thought doctor Oligo. By a stroke of divine luck reverend Randy had just read his mind but only in reverse tainted with a tinge of contradictions. "If men do have those capabilities of infinite power why can't they use it to cripple the powers of death? That way they can enjoy the eternity here on earth in the comfort of their homes and in the company of their families. And not wait for some esoteric delusion as phantom as heaven".

The thought of that as an answer tickled doctor Oligo's intellectual libido but unsuccessfully failed to jump-start his mission to find an antidote for death.

"What about your spiritual life?" The reverend re-minded him with a grin of smile.

"My believe in God fluctuates in sync with the state of my financial well being" Doctor Oligo answered with an edge of frustration. There couldn't be God in the context of human perception. Not with the degree of inequities and human demise going on. In Somalia, in Rwanda, in the middle east, in Uganda, in Nigeria, in Burundu. It can not be. The only reason why the church missionaries successfully foisted their idea about God on unsuspecting heathens is because they played on man's worst vice. Greed for wealth. Fear of death. The promise of eternity. Better life to come after death. Another place to find treasures of gold".

"Don't think that way doctor" the reverend begged him. Again, reading his mind. "Come see me in my office for salvation", he added only as a way to save his grace. The priest released doctor Oligo's hand only to pat his cheeks. Then he scuttled away to grab another masculine hand.

Settling down unto the residency-training program proved to be unexpectedly rigorous for doctor Oligo. He hated to walk the slippery rope of attending to 'in your face' patients and pleasing the boss's love for money. Nothing else mattered beside the bottom line. It was a cultural shock to him. But he learned quickly and held on tight. There were many occasions he wanted to walk away from the job. His endurance waxed and waned in sympathy with the common cold he was hired to combat. Gradually doctor Oligo had been reduced from an intuitive doctor that will clip the tail of death to an inner city disposable physician with his butt on the line.

Tons of endless lectures would be slated to talk about the cold virus. Life testimonies from victims were played on the tape over and over again. Ravaging winters were greeted with the understanding that more bucks will surely follow. One of the earlier lectures he attended was given by the allergist. He began ostentatiously: "Certainly you or someone you know has suffered from the common cold. Everybody knows how upsetting this can be. Suddenly you cannot catch up on your sleep. You are excusing yourself to get out for a protracted sneeze or to blow your nose. Making excuses why you cannot stretch out for a handshake or a kiss. Recollection of such events will probably send your countenance skidding momentarily down the valleys of depression. The inconvenience generated by such a little ailment can be staggering and your helplessness and hopelessness can soon be apparent in dealing with what seemed to be an easy walkover illness. If indeed adults can feel this way, imagine what the little fellows go through when they suffer from this ailment".

During his interview doctor Woeffry had warned him of the enormity of problems created by this ailment. It is now beginning to sink on him. Ever since he got into the residency program he has been dealing with victims of the common cold. He came into the training mentally charged to take on serious task of finding a cure for death but now he had been deflated by the ubiquity of an illness as trivial as a cold. He hated being asked to give unnecessary deliberation to the ailment. After all it is a self-limiting disease. He refused to consider that this might be all there is to medical practice in America. Listening to angry victims of the cold virus.

Not after seven long years in medical school. Not after those volatile embryology lectures. Not after fondling around with dead bodies for years. Interestingly their stories were compelling and captivating. It is a potpourri of cynicism blended with unfulfilled expectations. They sounded as if they were beaten by the Ebola virus.

When lunch break was over doctor Oligo returned to the clinic where he had completed a monotonous morning session of reassuring parents that the cold will eventually go away. He more or less expected similar afternoon session. He arrived just on time. The first set of afternoon patients were already in the examination rooms waiting for the doctors to move in. Rooms where assigned randomly to doctors as they arrive. He went into his assigned room, shoved his book bag into the desk draw, put on his white coat, hooked up his stethoscope, picked up the patient's chart from the desk and introduced himself to the patient and his mother, Ms. Marble.

For a second or two he stared on the chart again and back to the woman and her child. "What? A woman with a tale to tell about child's illness." It sounded to Oligo like a social worker's case. But he was not going to be judgmental.

"Hello Ms. Marble how can I help your son?" Doctor Oligo asked briskly, thinking it may still be an in and out case.

"My son had been beaten by the cold virus she answered"

"How did it start?" Doctor Oligo asked routinely.

"Where in the world do you want me to begin?" She asked. Then she took off with a narration that would have made an allergist go for a re-certification. "It all started on one miserable night. My son had returned home from school at about 4:30 PM with nothing but a few sniffles. So I gave him a warm bath and put him to bed early. Little did I realize what the night had in store for me? My husband works those 7 pm-7 am shifts, so he was gone for the night leaving me acting as a single parent. Playing the dual role of a guard and a doctor. My son coughed all night. Lying down tends to trigger a bout of cold, the so-called post-nasal dripping. He sneezed every three to five minutes. His nose ran nonstop. He mopped his nostril continuously with facial tissue and meticulously piled them up in the toilet. It was such a heap of tissue that by the time I went in to ease in the bathroom the only toilet in the apartment was clogged.

"Hold it there Ms Marble" doctor Oligo stepped in standing between Ms Marble and fast darting words shooting out from her mouth, "Please try to round up and tie together your son's problem ,we have a total of ninety seconds left to play with". He could have been talking to the ghost for all she cares. She continued more fervently. "Whenever bewildered I have a habit of opening the refrigerator. This time I had something in mind. Looking for left over medicine. One medicine bottle smelt like a familiar cold remedy. It's label was partially worn out. Luckily the remaining part revealed a current expiration date. So I administered one teaspoonful and waited for a miracle. Nothing happened for what seemed to be like an eternity. Thirty minutes went by and Jason—that's my son's name, seemed to have calmed down and was sleeping quietly. Coming only short of heart-beat-hearing distance I took a closer look at his face. A swollen sore red nose stared back at me. Both upper and lower lips were partially cracked. The skin overlying the corners of his left eyebrow was abraded. When I peered, I could see protruding flesh occluding the inner part of his left nostril. Good lord, What an illness. These words literally dropped from my gaping mouth. Jason must have been wiping too hard". She stopped momentarily to catch her breath for a while which gave doctor Oligo a false sense of freedom. But she was not going to be done so soon. "Exhausted from sleep deprivation, I turned to my watch to get an idea of how much time had elapsed. It indicated the time to be 3 AM. Almost simultaneously the little orange colored clock in the sitting room began to chime prompting me to take a breather next to the side window overlooking our neighbor's house. My soul searching and self-critic drifted temporarily. With random entropy it perched on vain materialism. Boy did they over-kill with the decoration. Their entire house inch by inch was wrapped in a glitter of scintillating light bulbs. Indeed Christmas was barely fifteen days away. Yet there has not been any glimpse of snow. Global warming is finally paying off. Not quite sure if this is good or bad".

The elasticity of doctor Oligo's patience had reached a breaking point. He hardly could take it anymore. This woman had plunged him into a state of homesickness. Reminding him of whom he actually is. Where he actually came from. What his mission was. It was all coming back to him. He could hear the crickets creak again, the native candles making a feeble imprint on the pitch darkness, the folks crawling out like rats to nimble on the remains of the dead. The children of Burundu leaning on the village darkness to hedge their way to the dug out toilets pits. What a contrast. What an inequality. Where is the cosmic order? Where is the Good Lord? The hour has come for doctor Oligo to turn a deaf ear to the woman's story. He has to disengage from her forthwith. Besides, the hospital official administrator has begun to signal him to tidy up for another patient. From the corner of his eyes he could see the official's sign language for time out. The frisking sound from his three first fingers indicated that time means money.

Doctor Oligo was at a lost on why Ms. Marble chose to reveal the details of her life in this fashion. He was supposed to be consulting for fifteen minutes only. That is the maximum time reimbursable allowed by the health executive managers from their last video conference meeting. The administrator is sure to ask the payroll to deduct the extra time spent from his paycheck. Loosing money not withstanding, something seemed to have glued him on his chair, listening to the woman's tale. Maybe he still has the vestiges of his Afro centric medical practice. 'In and out' is the rule of the game here. Unless he learned and masters it his job will be on the line.

"Achoooo ! Achoooo! I was jolted by a bout of cough and sneezing", the woman continued. "It was Jason again. Are you okay? Are you okay? I must have repeated this many more times. All my tender loving care was on display. Hugging, kissing, holding and carrying him. What kind of illness is this I kept asking myself? He is only two years old. How much suffering can a two-year-old endure? Again, I kissed him on the eyes, face, mouth, cheek, runny nose. As he lay on my chest I could tell that his heart was beginning to beat very fast.

"Wait a minute", she said abruptly reaching the road of adverse reaction. Doctor Oligo waited while she carried on some more. "Is a racing heart supposed to be part of this cold problem? Could an ordinary cold remedy cause someone's heart to gallop like a horse? Does anyone actually read those tiny prints on the label of those cold remedies?" All three questions were directed to nobody in particular. All answers parried by both parties. She differed thinking about such a calamitous possibility befalling upon her son.

That night as the woman stalled in action the little voice inside her began to talk. "Give Jason's doctor a call. Take him to the emergency room". She fumbled in her winter coat and handbags for the pediatrician's business card. No luck! Things are seldom available when you really need them. She hurriedly thumbed the yellow pages back and forth. Jason's pediatrician number was not listed. The little voice in her has now become uncontrollably loquacious. "You cannot figure this out anymore. Better take him to the emergency room. Call his grandpa or better still his grandma. Research about common cold in the Internet. Give Warner Lambert or Pfizer pharmaceuticals a call. Access a cold remedy hotline. Notify dad at work. Act now! Do something!

Quickly too".

4.

The first suggestion of taking her son to the hospital generated a manifest of inexplicable thought induced maladies. The closest hospital to where she lived is that of Silver Greek hospital. Chewing on the idea of taking Jason into this particular hospital left multiple canker sores in her mouth. Thinking over it sent a cold wave of skepticism down and up her spine. Sorting through this strange malaise laid open a sore wound in her bag of memory.

Hardly did any hour go by without security invited to separate a verbal or physical scuffle. For uncountable number of times a disgruntled patient or their relative will loose their composure, short circuits and spray venomous aspersions on the nurses, doctors and the hospital management. Isn't the hospital to the sick what the church is to the grieved? A place to find cure. A place of healing.

She could hardly reconcile the past with the present. She has been struck with a kind of dreamy state of mind. Apparition of children immersed in the stream of adult curses conjures up in her mind. With ease, archived information she thought and wished had been erased continue to download into her consciousness. Could she actually be remembering an event that happened when she was just three years old?

Seventeen years ago her mother had told her about an unforgettable night when she had to take her to a certain emergency room for a simple cold element. She was not even paying attention at the moment. So how did she recollect the incident in such a detail.

Fifty-nine other patients had to be seen before the doctor could take a looks at her cold After two hours in the waiting room baby

Marble was finally called to be triaged [medically debriefed] by a nurse and registered by the clerk. Following registration the clerk instructed Marble and her mother to go back to the waiting area until she is called to see the physician. Another six hours will elapse before the physician will see marble. Contact time between Ms. Marble and the physician was two minutes.

Diagnosis: common cold. "Your daughter has the common cold otherwise called 'URI' the doctor had said. "She does not require any medications. The problem will be gone in four to seven days".

Marble's Mother wasted no time in venting her feelings. She fumed that she spent eight hours only to be told that her daughter has the common cold. She already knew that she pointed out to the doctor. All she cared for was for a prescription. Antibiotic prescription. "None is required" the emergency room doctor repeated again. Marble knew for sure that her mother had acted out. Tore up her ER chart? Threw the chart in the garbage? Scratched a doctor in the face? Refused to vacate the exam couch? Must have been something fun because they attracted fleas of toothless hospital security men.

Doctor Oligo's next rotation took him squarely to the center of hospital fiasco, the emergency room. Ms Marbles tale served as a timely introductory lesson on what to expect. A prelude to his own ordeal. What he went through later on will forever change his focus on the rest of his medical practice. It sapped his mental energy and grounded his ambitions. His mission became a suspect. Gradually he had lost his inspirational prowess. Nothing cames to him anymore. Not when in the car driving. Not when in his room listening to music. His mind had gone barren. Dry of ideas. The kick in him hit a dead end. It is like somebody had transplanted his brain with that of a chipmunk. Gone are the days when inspiration rained on him like the waterfall of Niagara. Past are days when ideas crawled into his brain from every facet of his five senses. It really scared him.

He stretched out his neck to look beyond three years of residency sentence. He saw a glimmer of hope. Maybe things would be better then. Maybe everything will begin to come back to him. Maybe he would regain his freedom and latitude to pursue his goals. There wouldn't be any more doctor Woeffry grabbing him all over. None of that. None of his threat.

Surprisingly the department celebrated the end of the residency program with a prodigal party. In a brief speech read by the director he expressed thanks for all the doctors who delivered on the money. Warned that he wouldn't release the certificates of those doctors that failed to complete the patients claim forms.

While they were waiting for the dinner to be served, doctor Woeffry was called upon to entertain the audience. Quickly he rushed to the stage, unplugged the microphone from its stand and delivered one, two punches of some dirty jokes. He praised the gays and derided the straights. There was a rambunctious cheer for him as he began jacksoning his waist to the tune of the award winning rock and roll oldie 'rock the boat'. He danced to the right, twisted to the center and careened himself to the lap of one of the male resident doctors. Another cheer erupted from the occupants of the high table.

In reminiscent to his medical school graduation ceremony ten years earlier, certificates of residency completion were awarded. Each doctor stepped out from the audience to meet with the director of the program. Then the director would make some kind of remark about the individual.

Soon doctor Oligo was locked in congratulatory handshake with the director.

"This doctor worked very hard", the director testified, "however his hard work fell short of indefatigability. He does not seem to have any definable future ambition". What a sad remark. An ironic mischaracterization against someone contemplating on pulling a feat bolder than those of Napoleon Bonaparte and Alexandria the great combined.

Elevating from a resident-doctor-in-training rank to an 'Attending' is the status symbol any foreign trained doctor look forward to. You began to weld some authority. With that shred of power comes a stifling responsibility. It is a transformation that usher a new wave of tempest. All blames are hipped on you. Stories are concocted around you. When the hospital's balance sheet go belly up you got the blame. When the old man winter is tardy on its way, you get summoned by the department to explain why the patients stopped coming. All because the management did not quite believe you deserved to move from servitude to freedom.

Doctor Oligo felt that his preference was to work in the emergency room. This was the closest he could get to really making a difference between life and death. No other hospital care port of entry presents as much challenges. The tales speak for themselves. In the madness mix of patient care and making money there is no rule. Every corner has to be cut.

He worked the twelve hours, three days a week shift. To him it was a continuous period of fun and nightmare.

As an insider he began to capture the angle of medical practice as it was practiced in the Bronx. The work had taken a toll on him. He was now forty years of age. His height growth arrested at five feet nine inches. However he had added more adipose down the belly and up under the axilla. His eyes narrower exaggerating his sleepy look. Multiple groves had begun to line up beneath his lower eyelids. His shoulders sagged on both sides giving him a swaggering posture as he walks. His male pattern baldness was not helping either. Age seemed to have played a fast one on him. He had spent tremendous energy making and raising up two kids. One more is on the way.

The nearby gymnasium had been a place he had continued to pay visits. Eager to undo that which stress has done to his body. The sheet of large mirror pasted on the wall showed his full body contour all at the same time. Nothing to be proud about. He activated a tread mill and jogged on.

Someone had plugged in a tape in the over hanging television. It was one of those exercise motivational tape. Doctor listened as he worked-out. Everybody else was listening too. The gym was half capacity full. Fifteen different people with as many personality disorders. Pretty much regular patrons. Some obviously needed to be there. Others did not have any business in the world coming to the gym.

Doctor Oligo quickly made an eye survey to find out who is in and who was out today. Actually he was looking out for freaks. He found them interesting. There was always one or two at any given full session. The awkward gentleman to his right clearly needed to exercise—you do not need to put him on the scale. He is visibly overweight. He was going very fast and furious. You could discern the concern on the faces of other weight watchers.

"Are you certified in 'CPR'?" It was a familiar voice.

Doctor Olgo turned left, facing a young girl the size of a broom stick. Her face drawn so thin like that of a praying mantis. He counted her ribs through the hugging of her sweaty 'T' shirt. Her eyeballs buried in the prominence of her frontal bones. Her cheek bones stuck out as if in readiness for a bounce from a tennis ball. She looked ghoulish operated on a borrowed heart and brain.

Doctor Oligo survived the freight attack. It was the last living thing he had expected in the gym. His verbal synthesis was more effortless. He let the words fall from his lips as they formed from nowhere in particular.

"Hi Ms. Pinchomic, tell me why I must answer your questions. What are you doing here anyway? There isn't anything but your bones left for you to loose. Your presence is demoralizing those that really need to loose the extra pound. Do you get me?" Doctor Oligo emphasized.

"Because that guy on your right is a patient of doctor Ducey", Ms Pinchomic said ignoring doctor Oligo's question..

"You mean doctor Ducey the cardiologist?"

"Yeah, she said".

"Well my 'CPR' certificate expired a couple of months ago", doctor said feeling some ache from the curse of procrastination.

He suffers from—,she wanted to tell it all.

"Stop there", doctor Oligo objected. "Do not trample on Patient's confidentiality".

But I will be covered by the provisions of 'the good Samaritan law', the nurse debated him.

"No. Not at all, doctor Oligo informed her. "The law only applies in the case of emergency. There is none yet. The guy's lawyer would be all over you like a seasoned street brawler if you open your mouth a bit wider.

The big guy seemed to have gotten wind of the conversation. He slowed down on his exercise bike, stretched out his neck in order to catch a phrase or two. But it was too late. The conversation came to an abrupt stop.

Doctor Oligo seemed to have won the argument. And the anorexic nurse went on in full gear with her aerobics, tilting the steepness of the thread mill to 45 degrees and increasing the speed to 10.5 miles per hour. Her airy bone making only light impart beneath her feet. The body-trainer on the motivational tape seemed to have a grip on why some people get out of size. His approach sounded simple and easy to follow, even-though he looked fifty pounds overweight himself.

"People gain weight because they eat more calories than they spend, period. If you consume 2500 calories everyday but utilizes 2000 calories in all your body needs and activities, then the remaining 500 calories is stored for you in the form that increases your body weight. The way out, therefore, is to eat such that your calorie intake is commensurate with your level of physical and mental activities. Think about how trimmed you were when you were a teen. That is because you were restless both in physical and mental energy. All neat and straight. Both your thoughts and actions are on the move. You had no time to waste. Compare that stage of your life with your life inertia and drags as you get older. The worries erupt and carry with them foamy cheese of fat cells. And that is how you become overweight". That sounded very convincing.

"Did he say mental exercise is an alternative to physical work out in achieving weight reduction?" Doctor Oligo cannot take that assumption lying low. Here he is drenched in mental activities yet those irrepressible fat cells continued to creep up from underneath his skin. Mental drench got to be a positive contributor to weight gain. But how? Bulimic psychoses? Hormonal surge? No answer was forthcoming. Anyway his twenty two minutes exercise time is up. He walked out of the gym not quite sure whether he had actually gained or shaded any pound of weight. He promised himself to be back another day. In a matter of months his life compass swung a full 180 degrees. From a bespectacled introvert born with an irrepressible mission to let the dead man walk again, to a piece of disposable medical gadget with no agenda. He had paid his dues alright. He rose the rung from the bottom of the pit after escaping the depth of death in Burundu. Battled malaria and starvation. Passed through the rigors of cadaver dissection. Followed the shadows of his dream. Immigrated across the Atlantic to join his teachers in the new land. Whipped himself up to the top of the glass. Clinging on its inner lining like a lather. A pyrrhic victory with so many price to pay. Soliloquy has remained his only surviving pastime.

Day by day he continued to scale the dimensions on the map of his medical route. In a letter to his colleague down in Burundu he spilled the whole content of his bleeding heart.

Dear Doctor Haggler,

Please forgive me for the delay in writing you. Events have moved so quickly I could not believe I had been gone for so long. Days merge into nights and nights flow into days on end. I hardly keep track of the time anymore. How are you holding forth? Sometimes I do regret parting with you midstream from the boat of medical practice. I knew you would continue to paddle as strong as you can.

As you well know medicine failed me when I most needed it. May the clandestine hand of death never steal any of your patients. The apparition of my first professional mortality still torments me. The antidote I had sort all through my career continues to elude me. I have not even began to try. I do not know if I will ever get to it. I have been sidetracked by something bigger than death, life itself . I have to worry first and foremost about how to cater for my two little kids and their unborn sibling. Wiping their runny nose, changing their diaper and putting food on the table. You know how much I sought to wedge that war. To re-energize those dead batteries of cell through the hidden powers of breath. Instead I have been decimated by the force of economic demand to fight the cold war.

Currently I work at Silver Greeks, a hospital located in the heart of the Bronx borough. It is a hospital that caters to a considerable population of the urban poor blacks and other minorities. Unarguably descendants of our captured aunts and uncles that were sold to slavery hundred of years ago. It is a community in need. Maybe in as much dire need as our poor village in Burundu. Their shape and color of desire may differ a shade or two from those of our folks in the village. Nevertheless, it is a community in desperate need for help. They seek for it in their own peculiar way. With anger and misguided malice. Running the day to day hospital activities are doctors at various stages of residency training, medical knowledge and expertise. Foreign-trained medical doctors working as residents render most of the basic medical services. The resident doctors still in their specialty training are supervised by their more experienced counterparts called the 'attending' of which I am one. Thanks goodness. On a typical day this emergency room is like a circus with hundreds of the children and their parents swarming around a handful of resident doctors. Spiked {or if you like spiced} among them are one or on a good day two attending physician. Haunted by our inevitable faith. Worn out by our never-ending 'continuity of care'. We are at best defensive and apprehensive both in the practice of medicine and interaction with patients and their relations. This mal-adaptation may have originated from years of intimidation meted at the hand of certain clusters of virulent patients and their clones. Protected by the 'patient is always right' slogan. Propagated through generation of resident doctors. These particular group of health care consumers would do anything to embarrass the physicians that strives to provide care.

Critical questions, snickering remarks and blistering innuendoes are constantly thrown on our accents and cultural mannerism. Threats of mayhem are frequently made on our lives. Fragrant threats of lawsuits are rampant. With this shadow cast on our shoulders, we must continue to provide patient quality care. We do not really have a choice. Most of us escaped from poor third world countries in search of order, freedom and prosperity in America. If we were not ready to take the insult our more hungry brothers will sucker up for it.

Dialogue between us and the patients are clouded with suspicion. No matter how nice or concerned our medical team are, they tend to get pooh-poohed upon by some of the patients. Not long ago an observant nursing aide spotted an infant in a crib with rails down while the mother was walking away. The aide was quick to point out to mother about the potential dangers her child has been exposed to. But mother wasn't going to take the advice in good faith. "That is my baby not yours" was her mean reply to the aide.

Sometimes some days end up better than otherwise anticipated. Predicting on how each day is going to end is like walking the edge of a cliff. For some unexplained reason things have been much wackier recently. Almost every patient we attended to seemed grudgingly upset. Unapologetically so. Must be a kind of natural selection that has left us with a bunch of bad apples. Or perhaps the natural trend of water going the

way of least resistance.

Days are gone when we could actually count on some families not to mind the grueling waiting hours. To remain cool in the midst of perspiring aggravation produced in the emergency room environment. This group of patients have become extinct. Each day the doctors will be apprehensive on which member of the staff will be bullied. Newer staffs members tend to fall prey as their older colleagues master how to navigate the thorny medical road map in the emergency room.

Sights of female residents in tears following patient encounters are rampant. It reminds me of our days in medical schools when the ladies would cringe over the fright of cadavers. Please do not read this letter with so much sympathy for me. Do not shed any tears for me. My own tears will do. It flowed in abundance and had since dried up. I have since adapted to my new world like I did to the crickets creaking in Burundu. Like I accepted the uncertainty that I would never realize what my heart dreamed.

Convey my heart felt gratitude to my patients. For believing in me. For their understanding. For remaining supportive despite the shortcomings of my practice. In spite of the losses I encountered. For giving me the privilege

*to share in their most personal feelings. How clearer the differences have
become.*

> *Remember to visit my aging parents.*
> *So long,*
> *Until I write again*
> *Yours Doctor Oligo.*

With the letter clutched in his hand doctor Oligo drove to
the nearby postal office. Again he hesitated his exit from the car as
he listened to one of his favorite rock oldie. The music over, doctor
oligo began to turn the ignition key anticlockwise to cut off the
motor. He stopped midway. A commercial had come on at the tail
end interrupting the music. Amidst all that has been going on in his
life doctor Oligo could never understand the timing of the message.
Was it just a mere coincidence or as he liked to accept, the ultimate
hand of destiny. An underwrite that he is on the right pathway.

"Do you have a great idea? Are you being haunted by a great
idea? Wait no longer. Suffer no more. We are here to make your idea
become a reality—". Just exactly the kind of message doctor Oligo
needed to hear. He fished out a pen to scribble the contact number
hurriedly on his left palm before it leaks out from what has become
his basket brain.

By the powers of his elation doctor Oligo was levitated to the
branch office of "Current de Generale".

For the first time doctor Oligo had the opportunity to explain
his ideas to someone other than himself. The chief designer engineer
of 'Current de Generale' beamed two unblinking eyes on him
through the top of his glass frame while doctor Oligo frantically
scrambled for clay to mold body out of his sketchy imagination. He
was nervous. He adjusted his sagging shoulders. Tuned up his voice
to a good conversational tone and began to explain.

"My idea of 'inspigorate' is a devise about six inches long and
two inches or so wide depending on the laws of physics. Actually
size is of no practical consequence. The engineer did not seem

to mind his introductory gaffe. He went on. "The devise as I envisioned it has two ends or more, again depending on whether permissible by the laws of physics. One end of it should posses the capability to harness and store the last breath or the first breath or series of nascent breath a man takes. The middle chamber would energize the trapped breath, transforming it to 'enebreath' without destroying their delicate natural properties. The last compartment of the device would then deliver the 'enabled breath' at appropriate time through a predetermined point in a body part. Of course the appropriate time is when someone dies. An acupuncturist will help to identify the body site to be used. Through this one portal a quantum of natural breath energy is re-conducted to the entire human cell. The device is in an essence a sort of gentler, kinder, smarter shock paddle". The engineer showed no perceptible external emotions. So doctor Oligo went a step further. "For you to fully understand my idea sir, let us liken a human cell to a commercial storage cell, battery. A commercial cell is made up of a positive and negative sides. So also is the human cell which is the building block of a human being. Now, a storage battery has an expendable life which ends when all its charges are spent. Following the death of a commercial cell, we can either bury it, throw it away or re-charge it to restore back it's life. I dream of a day when we can do likewise to a human cell. I am determined to find a similar way to revitalize a human cell wherever in the body it is located. Whatever shape it has adapted to serve the body need. Of course in total due respect to the manner or time of death.

Recharging the heart, the brain to get back the soul. The muscle, the bones to get back mobility and sense of humor. The lungs to maintain perpetuity. The kidneys and bladder to get rid of toxins. The skin to restore beauty.

I am a thinker and a doctor. You are the engineer. You can take it from there". Doctor Oligo rested his swollen head on the fist of his hand and waited for the engineer to respond. The engineer's inertia was thicker than doctor Oligo had hoped. He must have been busy creating static electricity across his lips. He found his glasses, yanked it completely out from his face, removed his eye beam from doctor Oligo's visual field, adjusted the collar of his high profile "T" shirt, alighted form his swirling chair and motioned his hand for doctor Oligo to join him.

The engineer led the way to a show-case decorated with hundreds of weird inventions. Devices crystallized from the flakiest of murky ideas. He stuck out an acid chopped finger nail on the glass of the show-case to identify a device the size and shape of a medium size bicycle helmet. "Nobody knew we could do it when these idea was first broached to us. But twenty five years later the 'T houghtcerebrowizardromatic-analyzer' is nothing but a done deal".

"What does that do?" Doctor Oligo asked wondering if someone had beaten him to the punch. In total oblivious to doctor Oligo's eye popping reaction, the engineer continued in a very low key. "It reads peoples mind before they say the words, thereby eliminating loss of vital information between thought and spoken words. Scientists have estimated that more than fifty percent of a man's thought could be wasted in transit. The bottleneck is between the brain and the mouth. The phenomena have increased over the years resulting in the scarcity of intellectual wizardry. The likes of Socrates, Galileo, Bohr and Einstein. Secondly this 'TCW' saves a great deal of energy wasted in spoken words. Imagine how much energy you could have conserved if you had communicated all your ideas to me without saying a word to me?"

"Can you demonstrate it?" Doctor Oligo asked. He could no longer contain his curiosity.

The engineer picked the show-case lock with a secret combination code, retrieved the device from its own secured mini vault after another series of finger print combination code. Crowned his head with the device. It fitted him fine. Like a bicycle helmet without the chin buckle.

"Are you ready to play?" He asked doctor Oligo. "Not quite, doctor Oligo answered", making a deliberate effort to confuse the device The mumbo-jumbo of doctor Oligo's thought registered as unreadable in 'TCW' analyzer.

The engineer confronted him "Your thoughts are deliberately tortuous and incoherently hog-washed. No-body fools the thought wizard"

Okay, doctor Oligo admitted as he straightened up his thoughts. It displayed on the 'TCW' screen as an open book. Whoa! It was unbelievable, he said. He read the content of his thought with the engineer by his side.

"There is a chance that the human race would become extinct in the year 3000. Like the dinosaurs did. A lot of things could tip the human existence equilibrium into oblivion. Take a minute, think about it. What would happen if there was another bubonic plague. An Ebola or mosquito pandemic. A nuclear annihilation. What if by the year 2050 world death rate overtakes the birth rate".

"Is it in the market yet?" Doctor Oligo asked utterly perplexed at the accuracies of the device.

"No" replied the engineer. For a host of reasons. It is plagued by millions of law suits. People do not want their secrets made public or read by strangers. There was this unproven paranoia that the device would pull the rug off the media and news stocks. The device was also bugged down by cost, $1.5 million per unit".

Oligo's heart was now beginning to flutter with excitement. His own impending device is non-threatening to no one. He does not know of anybody who would want their neighbors or parents or children or bosses or even spouses for that matter to remain dead. If that other device can be conceptualized and created then his ideas could too. "Yes!", the engineer sounded as if he can do it. "Yes!, at least he did not think I am crazy".

When do you start and how long could we expect a test trial?" Doctor Oligo asked rapidly before the engineer could go into another attack of vocal inertia.

"You are looking at a minimum of twenty five years the engineer said. Yeah, quarter of a century. Our greatest challenge would be figuring out how to conduct your so called 'enebreath' through the delicate body proteins without causing liquefaction necrosis. Once we can handle that the rest will be easier. I am not saying a done deal, but easier", he emphasized. "With some luck I can dig up an old friend of mine, smart fellow. He is in his twilight. He is in the bioengineering field. He may wish to take the task as his valedictory project. We will get back to you in six months".

"Isn't six month a long time for a project as vital as this?" Doctor Oligo quipped. "It is going to be a hit. It would never threaten anyone. It would appease the conservatives since they love people so much and hated abortion more than vitriol. It would also give the liberals a second chance when that innocent black man or white man or colored man is put to death. Look at it closely, everybody is a winner. Besides this is not cloning. No hyper-kinetic strange new faces roaming down the street. Just the same old faces we are used to. Don't forget this not only for me and you but for the entire human race. From Africans to native Indians to Eskimos. People are dying as we speak. They are perishing in thousands. Real people. Important people. Clergies, teachers, cab drivers, rock artists, cops, psychics, strippers, presidents, princesses, chief executive officers, undertakers, Christians, Muslims, Jews, children, parents, doctors, senators, witnesses and alibi of innocent citizens in jail. Think about them". Oligo tried his best to cast his net far and wide. Still, no category of potential death victim seemed to strike a note on the engineer's emotional cord. Even the mention of the strippers failed to get a kick out of him. His affect was that flat.

Doctor Oligo continued to exert more pressure. "You need to give this project your topmost priority. I can help in the research. Even quit my job. It is all I had wanted to accomplish when I enrolled into medical school. Please shorten the time. Lets get started. Time is running out on human race".

Before the engineers lips could escape another attack of verbal resistance doctor Oligo's beeper went off. He read the message in disbelieve. "This is to remind you of your twelve hour shift this evening starting at 8pm. Please be on time. Enjoy your meeting. Personal secretary of doctor Gourji."

"How dare she bother me during my hours off?", doctor Oligo swore after reading the message. He has always been on time to work. More worrisome, was the transparency of the message when you read in between the words. How did the secretary know exactly where doctor Oligo was at that material time? Shortly he was catapulted back to the den of lions where doctors will be devoured by scores of frustrated patients.

5

The first of today's victim happens to be the chief orthopedic resident. Even his combined reliance in prayer and the mysticism of daily horoscope failed to foretell him of the impending horrific encounter.

Doctor Bernard Bonnya is not quite like any run-off-the-mill foreign-trained doctor on medical migration to America. At age fifty-two, he is a grandfather, has doctored in two continents and been honored in several intercontinental medical awards. His resume stretched impressively over thirty full pages. Containing accolades of brilliance, wit, compassion and indefatigability in the pursuit of patient care. Several honors have been pined on him that he only referenced recent ones. A man who is constantly expanding the frontiers of medical knowledge for the betterment of his patients.

He fled to the United State twelve years earlier when misfortune struck his country following the oust of the shah of Iran and the grip of power by a mob of Islamic militants. The option to flee over that of decapitation was a choice he had to make. Praying has remained his main source of strength as he transformed from one medical culture to another. As a back up against unforeseen events, he is an avid reader of daily horoscopes.

Whenever doctor Bonnya is on-call, medical staffs are happily relieved because he responds with dispatch. The emergency department needed him to consult on a seven year-old male who sustained a fracture while playing basketball. The two long bones in the kid's right leg were broken into several places. Dr. Bonnya had responded quite briskly. Gotten to the war zone within thirty second of his page. Not completely happy with the timing of the child's injury he insisted on obtaining direct information.

He usually enjoys talking with his patients. But this time, he was finished in such a short time. Something clearly must have gone wrong. As doctor Bonnya retreated back to the doctor's corner, his facial contour has noticeably drooped. Signaling loss of facial muscle tone from a deep seated emotional hurt. Tears well up his eyelids and drip down both his cheeks as tiny bubbles. He had been canned with the big end of a mother's stick.

Doctor Bonnya: "How come your seven year-old is playing basketball at two a.m. on a Tuesday morning? He should have been on his bed sleeping". His accent was so thick you can wedge a door on it.

Kids Mother: "Just do your job and mind your business. As a matter of fact, I do not appreciate advice from you alien doctors, which is why I did not intend to use this hospital facility in the first place. Blame it on the ambulance. They insisted on taking us to the nearest hospital, which happened to be your shitty hospital. Now can I get another doctor with no accent?" On listening to this doctor Bonnya's ego was bruised. He felt like cursing but couldn't find the right words. He had never experienced this kind of attack before. He was shocked with disbelief and frustrated by the negative reaction his questions had elicited.

Having hailed from an Aristocratic lineage in the Middle-east, respect is a given to them. No patient had ever been rude to him for the many years he spent practicing medicine in his own country.

It didn't take quite long before the incident reached the medical director. He quickly drafted a memorandum and enclosed in doctor Bonnya's paycheck The director had a penchant for coupling bad communication with paycheck. It was a way of reminding the doctors that their lives are tied up with the checks.

"Since time and places have changed, you too must change", the director wrote. "Dealing with this type of unprovoked bigoted invectives will be what you must endure if you will be around to complete your residency program in this institution. Please, always remember your emotion is of less importance and secondary to what we are trying to accomplish. Which is building a wider patient base and turning up profits. Any mistake we make is going to be capitalized upon by our competitors. Therefore you must not let your ego run so high. Keep it low. Very low".

With that kind of attitude coming from the top the battle ground is set for confrontations between the physicians and the patients.

Cuckoo! was the only way to describe the state of things happening in the emergency room this very day. In retrospect, the earlier group of patients that were seen sowed the jinx. Their cantankerousness jeopardized the doctors momentum to execute with speed and efficiency. The patients successfully tied up the two residents working with doctor Oligo on a twelve-hour shift.

Doctor J. Mesmere a second year resident, hailed from Bangladesh. Originally, he wanted a residency position in Psychiatry but had to do with pediatrics after three years of repeated trial.

Doctor Chikanery is a first year resident, a Senegalese. A carrier student who first spent seven years in the school of veterinary medicine. He later did additional seven years in the school of Homo sapiens because villagers were demanding that he consult on their children rather than their pets. Even his maternal aunt who suffered infertility for twelve years requested that he attended the delivery of her precious baby. It was quite a transformation. He eventually graduated with two medical degrees. He is nick named 'double D' in his village. For him the transition from pets to humans has not smoothened up completely. You can spot that out by his hesitation and extra caution when approaching patients.

"Only two residents and one attending to cover an emergency room of such enormous patient traffic? Unbelievable. They better be joking. Aren't they fully aware of how crazy this place can be?", Doctor Oligo asked hopelessly. "What is going to be their excuse this time around?" Probably the same old reason he has heard for so many years. Excuses that come from various levels. Packaged in different styles and shapes. Excuses that are familiar, unchanged and multiplying: Cost cutting. Reduction in the number of foreign trained residents. Hospital is on the red. The admission census is down. 'HMO' is hurting them. The nurses are threatening a strike. The hospital is settling sex molestation charges on doctor Woeffry. Doctors are not recording their procedures well. Doctors are not picking the higher code for medical billing. Failure to bill for doctor's spidery web scribbles. Over friendly weather condition. The cold bug is hibernating and has not struck big time. The ousted management was not billing on all services rendered. A money monstrous director has been hired to cut the fat pads off the girth of hospital expenditure. The Mafia has penetrated the rank and file of the hospital management. The neighborhood does not have many registered voters. They are politically dead. Name it, they have it printed and in flyers.

Meanwhile sweat had began to form tiny beads on doctor Oligo's visibly bald head. In five years he had turned from a hairy chimp to a bald eagle. Not a good sign. None of his family members is bald. His grandpa lived long enough to prove it. This job was beginning to take a toll on him. Six different articles yet for him to read on testosterone and male baldness. He has been carrying them around for months, but has not had time to read them. "There ought to be a better way of making a living" he admonished himself. What does it profit a man if he works this hard and die young.

The more patients they saw the more the patients trooped in. The three doctors combined seemed not to be making any kind of dent on those charts. Things were slipping away. They are at least six hours behind. The pressure was starting to mount. Time to really crank up the wheel and take care of this pile of charts. Otherwise the patients are going to take them hostage.

Good medical 'attendings' get kudos from nursing staffs and resident doctors because in moments like this they will double up their role and begin to see patients just like the resident doctors. This would be the litmus test for doctor Oligo. An opportunity to show how much and how fast he can crank the wheel.

6.

Guided by that spirit doctor Oligo temporarily jettisoned his supervisory role as an 'attending physician' and began to also see patients.

He went for a patient's chart. The microphone was conveniently placed beside the chart bin. He heaved a sigh of relief, leaned forward to speak on it. "Dead, dysfunctional, doctor". It was the desk clerk. Brief and direct no word wasted. If she wasn't stingy with words, she would have added, "get that bowleg of yours out to the waiting area and confront those parents face to face".

Separating the emergency room from the waiting area is a single security door to the north. Exiting the door emerged him face to face with a crowd of visibly vicious patients. About sixty kids waiting to be seen. More are still trooping in to register.

Before doctor Oligo could announce for the patient's name he was spotted by the two Physician assistants. They began to chuckle and hug each other. " I bet he is the new Attending" the dread haired 'PA' said. "He does not look like he could last for a long time here", the other gossiper concurred. They were loud and clear a deaf could here them. They were not hiding their skepticism. Doctor Oligo postponed his announcement and walked to them to inquire why he had attracted such glaring attention. "Why are you lasses laughing at me?" he asked. The PA'S answered him candidly. "Because nobody lasts here and we do not expect you to last either. The work here is brutal and the patients go for your jugular. Two Attending Physicians have quit in as many months. The dough is not worth the threats. You shall see."

Doctor Oligo refused to be coward into submission. Not so early. He wanted to give himself a fair chance.

"Please listen for your name". Daarlie, Daarliee. The sound of his voice was drawl and cracked more from fear than fatigue. It did not take long before his patient identified himself. The patient groggy from time wasted. Immediately, he wiped the smears drooling from the right lower corner of his mouth and headed towards doctor Oligo. Closely keeping pace with Darle is an older looking female companion. Some sort of facial resemblance. Turned out to be his sister. Nothing really peculiar with these siblings except that the sister was so closely in pursuit of Darle as if she was afraid he might fall or collapse. He looked pale and frail all right. His eyes appear subdued. His fingers slightly quivering.

'Syncope?' This must be a case of syncope, otherwise known as fainting doctor Oligo thought. It is a fairly common adolescent problem. Doctor Oligo love to play the game of visual diagnosis before getting to talk to the patients. It is called on-the spot diagnosis. After fifteen years in medical practice, ten of which were spent in Burundu, where the most sophisticated medical equipment available was a stethoscope, doctor Oligo's clinical acumen is sharper than a laser beam. Most of his on-the-spot presumptive diagnosis is right on the money.

"Room number five. Have a seat in room five please, I will be with you in a moment", doctor Oligo instructed. As his patient was waiting he asked the desk clerk to activate the hospital administrator for a diversion. In other words the emergency room would no longer be able to accept critically ill patients. Doctor Oligo wanted the ER administrator to notify all the ambulances and paramedics. His staff and resources are stretched beyond limit and unless a patient was dropping dead in the next minute the average waiting time is six hours. To avoid any confusion in medical lexicon, he wanted every letter of every word spelt out to the administrator. For non-emergent cases where time is of no concern the patients are welcome to wait as long as it takes. Which is probably the end of time. The medical crew was not ready to explicitly tell anybody to go home and soothe their cold with disposable tissue and hand washing.

Now back to his patient. "Hey buddy, how are you today". Doctor Oligo introduced himself simply as doctor 'O'. He did not want to further upset the adolescent by bugging with his full name. "What can I do to help you?", he asked. But doctor Oligo's glaring attempt to create rapport faded when the patient's sister spoke. "Didn't you read his chart?", she queried . "Give him something for cough. That is all he needs. For your information we have been waiting for six hours in your emergency room. Six full hours and counting. So, mister make it snappy"

"Well sorry about that" doctor Oligo apologized. "We are kind of short on resident doctors today. I wouldn't waste any more of your time. Why not go on and tell me what is going on. I will try as much as I can to get you out of here very quickly". The sister's iced heart watered a bit and she added a few more words to fill the doctor in on the case.

"Darle has been smoking three packs of cigarette everyday for six months. Lately he has been coughing and spitting blood". Her story hit an abrupt stop when she mentioned the word 'blood'. "Now will you give us the prescription so that we can leave?"

Fired up about the unsuspected turn of event, doctor Oligo began gathering his needles and syringes for investigation and perhaps admission. Possibly a case of tuberculosis or early smoke induced lung cancer. Leaving no stone unturned he simultaneously began to educate the patient on the dangers and harms of smoking.

"Enough of your sermon Mister, we have heard all that before". It was the sister's hawkish voice again. "If you don't give us any prescription we will be out of here in a jiffy".

Pushed to the wall but still eager to negotiate, doctor Oligo made his final truce, knowing fully well that he may be close to unraveling something, which can make a huge impact on the health of the entire community. "Take this form" he said handing the patient an x-ray form. "On your return from the x-ray you can have a prescription for cold and cough medication. It is over the counter anyway", he added. Doctor Oligo's plea was handed in the most amicable way with gestures and gesticulation.

That must have ticked off the two siblings. "Dress up, let's go" the sister barked in a military tone. And in a robotic motion, the boy sat up from the examination couch, shoved his hands into his sleeves, zipped up his pant, latched his sandals and was ready to leave. In no time they were opening the door that led to the street. Doctor Oligo watched in catatonic consternation.

On their way out the exit door doctor Oligo heard the swear from the boy. "Mister, next time you walk the street better watch your back". Too bad, no time to sulk or call his wife to let her know of the impending danger in which he found himself. He was terrified of dying knowing that he has not been able to find an antidote for death. Worse still, apart from the engineer nobody else knew about his thoughts. And he did not feel that the engineer has shown enough commitment to bring his ideas to fruition. It wouldn't be the best time for him to die. "Lord, not this very day he prayed".

The situation in the ER was really getting berserk. None of the staff was having a good day or getting a handle over the pile of charts. Sheer determination was the only thing left in doctor Oligo to carry on. "Next time, do not be overly concerned or over-friendly" he admonished himself. "Just detach from your patient. Careless on what they do or say to you. Ride on doctor. Welcome to this neighborhood. This is the way it has always been and this is the way it will surely remain. But this job has to go on. To be daunted is an act of cowardice".

His second patient happened to be a four and half year old male with attention deficit hyperactivity disorder. Even though doctor Oligo tried to keep him at arms length, the lad was hell bent on making his presence painfully memorable. He wrestled an otoscope from doctor Oligo's hand. Double jumped with it from the examination couch to doctor Oligo's back. At that vantage point the lad began to suffocate doctor Oligo with the stem of his stethoscope. Oligo's face turned pale and his mouth gasped hungrily for breath. "Open your mouth wider for me doctor", the kid tormented the doctor. Desperately doctor Oligo tried to shake the kid off. He must have been a little bit out of balance. The kid's weight sent him reeling over the open pack of laceration kit on the Mayo stand. Everything on it came crashing unto the floor. Needles, scissors, antiseptic liquids, forceps, adhesive tapes, band-aids and a pair of alices forceps all of which where discarded into the sharp container.

The patient's mother who was a witness to all this unfolding drama chose to remain unfazed and un-interfering. "This is exactly what I am going through twenty-four hours a day seven days a week" she finally mumbled. "The Ritalin seems to have given him more energy. He needs something stronger".

Soon after escaping death by strangulation, doctor Oligo was ready to continue with the care of this patient. "All right, you hold him while I do a quick physical exam on him", doctor Oligo begged the mother. "No sir", the mother snapped. "You have to call your people to come and hold him. I just completed bilateral hip replacement and this daredevil is working hard to undo it".

It took two male nurses and an aide to hold the boy steady while doctor Oligo leaned over to take a peak in his ears. Regrettably they forgot to guard his mouth. As soon as the doctor bent over the lad squirted about five cc of watered saliva across his face. And in the pandemonium he freed himself. Doctor Oligo had no choice but to take it as another of the day's several mishaps. Some kind of professional hazard. That is one of the beauties of being a doctor in this neighborhood. The patients give you all they have. Right from the bottom of their guts.

Doctor Oligo took a couple of minutes to calm down his nerves. But his neurons wouldn't stop firing . At the right hand corner where asthmatic patients receive nebulizer treatments, a heated argument was on the way between a female intern and a parent.

"Try another hospital for a second opinion if you do not like my diagnoses", the female doctor said.

"This is the Bronx not Russia, you bitch" the parent replied. He was screaming and was so close to the doctor's face that doctor Oligo thought the parent was going for a head butt. "And let me remind you this is our hospital and we can make whatever demand we want. Without our Medicaid money you wouldn't have a job".

Doctor Oligo took his eyes off the scene not wanting to attract attention to himself. After all he received enough insult for the day. But the bang on the glass window forced him to gaze towards the clerk desk adjacent to the window.

"How can I help you? the clerk asked the heavily set man.

"When am I going to be called to see the doctor? the man asked?

"I gave you that answer less than minute ago. The doctors are running late. It could take between four to six hours. The doctors are battling with a very sick patient. Be patient and they will get to you soon as they can".

The clerks explanation did not seem to move or acquiesce the man.

"We got to be seen anyway. My daughter have not made doodoo for over a week" the man said.

"Well I cannot help you on that. Is there any other thing you want me to do for you", the clerk inquired.

"Kiss my ass" the man shouted and left.

Despite the entire hullabaloo, a mini-round must be conducted by the medical team led by doctor Oligo as the supervising doctor. The purpose is to create awareness based on positive identification of patient status as well as the level of care provided by their assigned physician.

Doctor Chikanery was tied up with that case of diabetic ketoacidosis. Good progress. Patient is doing well. The normal saline bolus had gone in. Insulin drip has been on for an hour. Patient is becoming less acidotic. Good sign, but not out of the woods yet. He is still hungry for air. His breathing continued to be less deep and rapid. They had begun soft-landing on the fluid replacement.

The appendicitis case was ready to be taken to the operating room. The transporter was waiting. Thank goodness, at least one mission is nearing accomplishment..

Room number four was an easy case of west Nile encephalitis scares. There were only a few mosquito bites on the extremities. No headache no fever, no lethargy. Nothing worth worrying about. Send him home, doctor Oligo instructed the assigned resident.

Room five was a "no tell case". A sixteen year old female stabbed on the neck, a hair breadth short of the jugular vessels. She is lucky to be alive. But there was a problem, she is not telling. She has refused to implicate the assailants. No names. No motives. Absolutely giving no leads. The cops as well as the physicians were perplexed.

Getting to room five was an impossible task in itself. A pool of vomit covering a two-meter radius had been sitting there for more than three hours. House keeping is being sought at every nook and corner. A manhunt had been declared. At last check, the house cleaner remained at large. The last time anybody sighted him was at the beginning of the shift, which was approximately eight hours ago. He had shown up on his own to announce that he was the only one covering the entire hospital sanitation and laundry needs. "Therefore, do not expect miracles" He had warned.

The pool of vomit barred the medical team from making eye contact with the rest of the patients. Identification was made by finger pointing across to their respective rooms.

In attendance for the mini-round were two medical students, the two physician assistant, the head nurse, Ms Bird, a social worker, doctor Chikanery and doctor Oligo. Doctor Mesmere was no where to be found. Usually anybody in the line of patient care is mandated to join in the round. But where the heck is doctor Mesmere? Doctor Oligo asked again to nobody in particular. Ms Bird stepped in to answer his question. "He is still dawdling with that blood pressure measurement. This is going to be the tenth time he will be wrapping that undersize cuff over the poor girl's arm. Trying to dispute a 5mm-mercury difference initially obtained by the triage nurse. Multiple repetition can only be one thing. Obsessive-compulsive disorder. An effort which is not going to pay off in this emergency room period. He could have been better off sticking with his first love of training in psychopathology".

"Okay, Ms Bird let doctor Mesmere know that I want him to stop any further recheck of that blood pressure", doctor Oligo said. In silence however he wondered if she hadn't gone overboard in doing some check on doctor Mesmere's mesmerizing background. Besides, how else did she know this much about him? That he had a stint with psyche.

By choice doctor Oligo failed to give much impetus to the nurse's charge. A way to disallow the incident from escalating into another impromptu staff meeting. But his verbal actions failed to pacify the head nurse. She continued with her outrage, eager to drink out of doctor Oligo's blood.

"Patient is getting hurt with all that arm constriction. Some petechiae is beginning to develop around her upper arm. Why not ask doctor Mesmere to have this patient followed in the clinic? She demanded. Patient is stable, talkative and obnoxious. Beside she is here solely to check out if she is pregnant. And thank goodness nothing is showing in the pregnancy kit".

Officially the round is over and doctor Oligo must continue with the rest of the patients. He promised to catch up with doctor Mesmere as soon as possible to determine exactly what is going on between him and the patient. Barely three hours later Ms Bird returned back to doctor Oligo clutching a bag of peanut and a baggage full of scoops. How busy she has become prying into other staff activities.

Doctor Oligo was really beginning to get unease that Bird was still perching all over him despite his persistent attempt to shake her off forever.

"What is on your mind ms Bird?", doctor Oligo asked pointedly. Before ms Bird responded she dipped into her peanut bag, selected a peanut and punished it in between her left molars.

"Do you have a couple of minutes she inquired?" Having no problem talking as she munches. "Not really", doctor Oligo said with an edge in his voice. "Just be as brief as you can be. Cut the chase right to the bone". He abhors her habit of talking while munching peanuts. It trivializes even further whatever gossip she has to tell.

Aside from being a head nurse, Ms Bird is at least two other things. The harbinger of bad news. And the self-appointed emergency room puritan. If you were an attending physician in-charge of a busy emergency room do not sublet to her because she will flood your time with trivial complaints and reports. It seemed that she was solely programmed to sniff for doctor's oversight and omissions. She kept tag on what the doctors did as a group and as individuals. What time they signed in and out. How long they spent on medical round. How often they gathered for spontaneous exchange of medical ideas. Recorded how many times they went to the bathroom while on the job. Reported how many personal visits or calls they received per day. Commented if anyone of them had not mastered their vene-puncture technique. Rated on them if they were making too many of the same diagnosis. Picked on them if they were using too many of the same brand of antibiotics. Quick to offer a gum, another way of telling them that their breathe smelled. She noted when they were using a borrowed stethoscope. Wrote them up for forgetting a cotton swab after a patient exam. Screamed foul play if she spotted any of the doctors asking for a spare pen to write with. Conducted post conferences on their patients solely to elicit how they hated the doctors or misunderstood their accent. Rumor have it that she passed this information line hook and sinker to the director for a kiss of weird favor. Everybody watched what he or she said or did whenever she was beside, behind or beneath them.

"Did you say a possible case of malpractice?" Doctor Oligo wanted to make sure he heard her right. "It could well be" she answered. "Blood is oozing non stop, difficult to say whether the tympanic membrane is ruptured or not", she added bouncing allover doctor Oligo's elevated anxiety. A piercing silence followed while doctor Oligo regained his leadership focus. Without her spelling it out he knew that doctor Mesmere is doing his thing again.

"How many human parts is this guy going to have a crush on. Digging a toddlers ear for damn wax? Never worth the trouble. It is called cerumen. Everyone has it in their ears. A drop of diluted hydrogen peroxide is all you need. Debrox ear drop if you want to be very impressive. It is only a matter of time before this guy drags me in front of the jury to account for my supervisory role as an attending physician". Everybody knew that doctor Mesmere had been acting weird since doctor Woeffry took him in his wing as his preceptor. Recently he had developed a tendency to constantly look over his shoulders. Very much withdrawn to himself. Something must be going on with him hanging around doctor Woeffry.

Doctor Oligo wasted no time to issue a steep warning to doctor Mesmere through Ms Bird. "Please tell doctor Mesmere to stop everything he is doing forthwith. To stay far away from that patient and from any other patients for that matter. To document all that he has done so far". Doctor Mesmere was not to see any other patient until doctor Oligo reviews his preparedness and state of mind.

Hoping his elaborate statement concerning this matter would do it for their heated discussion, doctor Oligo made a physical effort to extricate himself from Ms Bird. "Can I quickly attend to another equally pressing problem before I catch up with doctor Mesmere?" he pleaded with Ms Bird. He had no doubt in his mind that she was just using him as a convenient catharsis for her pressurized stress. He couldn't figure out why she was rushing him into so many search and frisk operations at her own pace.

Problems will always inundate this emergency room unless management stopped seeing the medical staff as stacks of money machines. Doctor Oligo would rather tackle these problems conveniently in order of priority and not let someone else shove them down his throat. The dose of it had caused his facial frown to deepen and his pinched nerve to begin firing. At no time did his job contract include acting as a Dick. His displeasure was clearly translating into somatic symptomatologies.

7

In total disregard to doctor Oligo's objection, Ms Bird carried on with her gossip. "Listen doctor, you must hear this one. Lend me your ears and you will be glad you did." Her voice barely perceptible as she began to masticate a rare twin peanut. "What again? What? What happened?" She sure knew how to recapture doctor Oligo's attention. What could it possibly be? Awe inspiring enough to tame Miss Bird's powering voice into a whispering low?

His patience was wearing thin. Had someone collapsed from fatigue while sitting in the over-crowded waiting room? Is the kid who scared the hell out of him lurking in the shadows with a sniper's rifle? He couldn't wait anymore. He seemed to be saying to Ms Bird "please give it to me now before you throw me into a shattered wreck". He hated suspense.

The news finally ejected from her mouth. "Somebody slapped the director across the face. One of the women did it". A bombshell news indeed. It hit him as if he was the director reliving the attack.

Urgently doctor Oligo needed to clarify the event with a series of question. "Wasn't the director supposed to be home at the time the incident happened ? Did he fight back? I mean smack back? Is this a case of Karma?" Not long ago this director was none perturbed to a case of resident abuse. It looked like he had met with the same treat. From the feedback extracted from Ms Bird, doctor Oligo was able to knit together a skeletal chronology of what happened.

At about three in the morning news had been passed to the director that there was chaos in the emergency room. So he drove in to take a look. He then got into a loop argument with a patient's mother. The director and mother went back and forth like a hula-hoop for fifteen minutes. The director unable to disentangle himself got smirked on the cheek.

"Interesting, isn't?" Nobody has seen this one happen before. News of resident doctors being smacked here and there no longer made it to the coffee shop gossip corner nor to the grand-round conferences. Resident and attending doctors having their pants and dresses ripped do not make a breaking news anymore. Nor does the management raise an eyebrow when the doctors are spat on. But talk about a medical director being slapped around on the cheek like dough, that is a novelty. A macho director for that matter, with chest the size of a double swinging doors. His neck a constant abode for priceless jewelry that would prompt any jewel store to go for a hostile takeover bid. He carried himself so high on the air of empty arrogance. The words on his office door stated that loud and clear "the best director money can buy".

"Did he identify himself?", doctor Oligo asked. "I wouldn't know" Ms. Bird replied. The question of who had the bravado to hit director Gourji was too intimidating for doctor Oligo to ask. You bet it was Ms Applewhite the delirious demimondaine. One of the arrant client. She was like a time bomb waiting to explode. Her voice was still resonating across from the hallway as she challenges the next daring physician to come forward and get poked in the eyes. No one took the bait. She paced up and down the mini hallway next to the ER, totally out of control. Security was called to rescue the situation. In a matter of minutes she was semi-circled by five big men.

"Freeze!", she shouted. "Do not come near me unless you want to get hurt". They obeyed her and maintained their distance. The director has recovered from the beating but still mad with this apparently unprovoked attack. Seeing the security standing akimbo he ordered them to avenge, to attack and to make her pay. But he was not going to be able to incite the security to be physical with Ms. Applewhite.

Unhappy with their lack of counter offense he instructed the desk clerk, Ms. Tan to inform the closest police prescient about the incident. "Ask them to respond pronto. Let the desk sergeant understand that director doctor Gourji needs the finest of the bravest to come to his aid."

Applewhite was bracing for the cops. She continued with her tirade. Swearing obscenities with her daughter. Entertaining the mini crowd that had flocked to cheer her to victory. "I have been coming to this emergency room long before some of these residents thought about getting into medical schools" she announced. "Long before some of them stopped wearing diapers." Again, the crowd chorused in support. Sure she is right in a way if you want to give her credit despite her atrocities.

It didn't long before the riot spread to erupt other patients. The ER director had been pummeled into submission. The security staffs had been paralyzed. All the protective defenses broken. The patients now moved in to take the medical infrastructures one by one.

A thick set teenager ran into the wall, gathered enough momentum and body slammed on one of the physician assistant. She passed out and began foaming from the mouth.

A faked hair Blondie went to the chart bin to look for her records. She found it only to shred it. Finally she went to dispose of it in the garbage. In the process another woman spotted her chart, stuffed it in her hand bag. She picked up the bin and used it to smashed the ER computer screen. Satisfied, she walked away.

A grandma had one of the medical students in an arm lock threatening to smolder him if he continued with what she called 'too many unnecessary questions'.

A patient waiting since twelve hours for admission tore off his heplock and dripped blood allover the floor.

For undisclosed reason a mob of angry patient relatives were hell bent on locating doctor Oligo. They had his named written in red ink on a piece of dead leaf. But thank goodness Ms Bird had him restrained listening to her stories.

After the incident the hospital administrator on duty came in to apologized to Ms Applewhite for loosing her temper. "You doctors must learn to work very fast", he scolded the doctors. "Attend to these patient fast enough and you can avoid being smacked on the face. Give them what they want. Give them antibiotic prescriptions for the sake of peace and tranquility."

Thereafter Ms Applewite brought her daughter to the emergency room for anything imaginable. She brought her if she needed antibiotic for a cold sniffle. If she hadn't moved her bowel for twelve hours. If she needed the doctors to put the infant to sleep. If she cried with no tears. If her asthma medicine was about to finish. If it was a holiday and she needed a box of diaper, a pedialyte or some baby formula. The residents hated consulting on the chart with that name. They toss the chart around until some brave unsuspecting doctor came around.

Finding another hospital that would tolerate her as the doctors in Silver-Greek hospital did wasn't easy. She was reportedly booted out and refused treatment in one of the lofty nearby hospitals unless she shades all her attitude. But it is quite the opposite here at S and G hospital. In a recent memorandum posted on the notice boards, the director was quoted as saying "she must be tolerated" with the word 'must' was underlined multiple times.

Doctor Oligo shuffled his teeth when he read the memo. "How come we are stuck with her?", he asked intuitively. He got the answer. "Perhaps, you do not deserve any kind of respect. You are treated as desperate immigrants who do not have any options other than to eat from the middle of the sharp containers. The alternative would be to starve".

This is real. Not a figment of his imagination. He felt certain about that. The majority of the doctors here are not permitted to get jobs in areas of their choice. They got to work in the so called medically underserved areas. A fetid misrepresentation of human medical need.

The more ground Ms. Bird broke in getting out her stories the more she demanded.

"One last thing if you don't mind doctor Oligo", Ms. Bird said looking at her watch. "My break is in three minutes. I got to let this one out quickly", she added as a matter of fact. "But Ms Bird you do realize how backlogged we—" doctor Oligo began.

It is amazing how quickly Ms. Bird recharges for yet another episode of bad news. Quick wit had never been doctor Oligo's greatest virtue. He had no chance to contemplate on Ms. Bird's request. Her sharp tongue had perfected the art of intrusion. As doctor Oligo paused, Ms Bird continued already trapping another pea-nut for onward sentence to eternity

"Guess what? Boy Levee is back. Dad brought him back, and wants him admitted. Wouldn't take no for an answer." "But I discharged him two hours ago", doctor Oligo screamed. Anybody close enough could notice the huskiness in his voice. "Today is the wrong day for Mister Levee to be playing this hanky-panky game in the Emergency room". Things were definitely slipping out of their hands and he did not need any more of this unnecessary distraction. "Well doctor I am afraid he has been threatening to get in touch with his attorney. You have to handle this one. I do not want any piece of it", she said. "Wait a minute Miss Bird", doctor Oligo said. "What am I going to admit him for? I had listened to his chest before, his lung was as clear as a whistle. No medical reason to keep him on the hospital hotel. Look at him prancing around like a matador with a Popsicle in his mouth and a musical headgear. I can tell one mile away that he is not wheezing".

"Yes my boy is wheezing." Levee's father has crept in from nowhere to fight doctor Oligo's medical assessment.

Determined to settle this matter quickly without any further ado doctor Oligo asked him to bring in Levee so that he can listen again to his chest with a stethoscope.

"Good to see you Levee what is going on?" Doctor Oligo wanted to be as unruffled as possible. "I am back again" he answered. "Are you wheezing?" The doctor asked. "Yeah I guess, very bad" Levee said. And he proceeded to generate some phony wheezy sound. Externally he made his nares to flare and labored his respiratory chest muscles to move in and out. By so doing he provided the perfect text book description of severe acute attack of asthma.

Oh yes, doctor Oligo has seen boy Levee do this deceptive maneuver hundreds of times over. At age fifteen boy Levee held the record for the most hospitalized child on the pediatric floor. Three hundred admission and still counting. May be some kind of psychosomatic disorder or Mauchausin syndrome by proxy.

Discounting his five feet short stature, boy Levee was sculpturally handsome. His narrow mouth with thin lips, fitted to a prominent bridge of nose, which in turn fitted perfect with a dolichocephalic shaped head. Inside this mold of passive facial contour are two darting marble glass eyes. The two eyes combined made his being come to life and conquered what could have easily pass for a manikin at a apparel store.

As soon as the father realized that doctor Oligo was inclined to discharge levee, he began throwing a fit.

"Repeat your name for me", Mister Levee demanded. "Oligodendroglier, Oligo for short" the doctor complied. "Oligo what?" Mr. Levee demanded again. "Dendroglia", doctor Oligo told him. "Spell it out" he insisted. The doctor spelt out the sixteen letters of his name. Mister Levee followed up with a series of questions; "What sort of name is that? Who gave you that name and for what? What medical school did you attend? When did you think of becoming a doctor? Were you taught about asthma? How many times did you attempt your board exams? When did you arrive in this country? Are you sure you are legal? Can you show me your green card? Did you attend the last national conference on asthma? Has my attorney talked to you yet?" He carried on for another ten to sixteen minutes. Puffing and doodling as he conducts an unauthorized interrogation on doctor Oligo. He obtained enough dossiers on him to shame any prospective biographer. His purplish face showed the degree of exertion he spent quizzing doctor Oligo.

When he came short of his last breath doctor Oligo had a window of opportunity to reaffirm his decision on boy Levee.

"There is no need for admission Mr. Levee. Your son is fine. Take him home. Feel free to bring him back for re-evaluation anytime". Thereafter he excused himself to run to another troubled spot.

A complaint line of patients and their sympathizers covering a ten meter distance had formed. Call it a pressure group demanding for doctor Oligo's entire head and attention. They were all interested in talking only to the head doctor. Each complainant apparently wanted to convince him that their child was the sickest and ought to be seen before any other patient.

Listening to everybody with problem was an onerous job. So doctor Oligo decided to lend his ears to only a handful at a time.

The first complainant chose to use her time to question doctor Oligo's authenticity. She leaned forward to peer into his hospital badge. "You are an Attending" she declared. "Yes I am" doctor Oligo agreed. "So get us a real doctor", the woman lashed out. "We wanted to deal with a real doctor and not an Attending."

Since doctor Oligo had been through a similar confusion before he was rather amused than offended. He realized that lots of explanation is part of this job. "I am neither an 'Attendant' nor a 'Pretender', but an 'Attending' which means a physician in a supervisory role".

Next, a very concerned man introduced himself as the foster parent of a four year old girl. "My daughter is in a lot of pain" he said. "She has ammonia" he said. "That is what she suffers from. She has been admitted three times in the past for this ammonia". Nobody noticed the slip, but he was actually referring to a case of pneumonia and not "ammonia"

Last complaint was a case of 'chicken pops'. Rash is something the physicians deal with especially in pediatric practice. When it pops out dramatically it can be confused with a case of 'chicken pops' instead of chicken pox.

Every now and then doctor Oligo thumbed through the piles of the accumulated charts. To make sure no real emergent cases had slipped through the split or had been relegated to the bottom based on mere registration time alone. It is also an opportunity for him to be aware of the variety of the cases held up in the waiting area. In most instances nurses' triage note will pretty much give an idea of the cases that are brewing.

A total of sixty five charts in the box. Counting case by case, there were 6 cases of rash, 1 case of complication from tongue piercing and a case of hurt coming from a belly bottom ring. 7 cases of wheezing, 2 cases of bicycle accident, 4 cases of fever, 18 cases of cold with runny nose. 2 'home alone' cases and 1 case of a beer bottle in the rectum. Two girls came in to check if they were pregnant. There was 1 possible case of appendicitis,4 cases of ear pain, 2 patients needed to refill their seizure medication, 1 case of sexual molestation, a couple of vomiting and diarrhea,2 cases of constipation for a week, 2 cases of school clearance letter. 1 kid came in for stitch removal. 2 kids came in because "their mother wanted them admitted." Apparently she had an important party to attend and wouldn't afford to pay a baby sitter. There were six or so walkouts.

There was a case of possible knuckle fracture. That of a fourteen-year-old male who got upset and decided to take revenge on the wall.

Among the so many charts, two needed further considerations. A case of death on arrival 'DOA' seen earlier this morning? A twenty three years old man found dead on his bed in the morning. Doctor Oligo quickly separated the chart from the rest of the bulk. Took some time to reflect around it.

Something about this case flicked a switch in the doldrums of his complacency. For a change, he felt the grip of a powerful hand pulling him away from what appeared to be the shackles of an entangled cobweb. Initially the destination was fuzzy as one previous page of sunset receded to a new glowing page of sunshine. Doctor Oligo tried his best to maintain a balance of his wobbling feet. A phrase conjured up and replayed endlessly across the breadth of his remembrance faculty; "who gave you that name and for what, who gave you that—." The transformation ended. Oligo woke up and tried to extrapolate his orientation. Behold, he had been set back on his track. Back on his mission. He was lost but now he has found his way again.

"What a perfect case for 'inspigorate', he said with a sigh of vindication. "Young man, no prior illness. Perfect pre-morbid health. Got to hospital on time. Simple shut down of the body cell batteries". He knew with certainty that a device such as his envisioned 'inspigorate' can make this man come back to life. No doubt about it. But there was a problem. No feedback from the engineer.

"What the heck is taking this 'Current de Generale' company so long to get back on my project?" he asked tearfully. Obviously, when it came to a dead man's misery they did not see beyond their bottom line. All they see are; End of another era of generativity. Passage of wealth to close family members. Inheritance galore. Death tax that would ameliorate national debt. Nature's own way of trimming population explosion, getting rid of the society's poor. God's retaliation on man's sins. Bumpy harvest for the funeral homes."

Doctor Oligo stared for the tenth time that day at his wrist watch. One hundred and eighty days is indeed a long time. One week, two hours, five minutes and twenty two seconds. That's how much longer he must wait before he gets a feedback from the engineer. The way things were going he probably needed the last second of the last minute to communicate back to him. Just to make a decision on a life and death matter. No matter how much time the engineer took, his idea was going to be a make or break moment in the history of mankind. A land mark far greater than the renaissance, the industrial revolution, the abolition of slavery, the advent of vaccine and antibiotic, the complete sequence of gene.

Why are they treating the idea with a kid's glove? Is it just a matter of pure economics or man's fatalistic submission to death? Perhaps the venture capitalists had determined that his product would not be cost effective and that his idea was crazy. How dare them. They know nothing about medical science. They never had the opportunity to dine and sleep with cadavers. That could explain why they would never get back to him. Couldn't be, or could it? His mind re-assured him that his reasoning was logical.

If man can regenerate a commercial battery cell, why can't he regenerate a human cell.? How long was it going to take for someone to figure out how to conduct the breath of life across the proteins, the carbohydrates the lipids all in a linkage handshake to build man. It may take time. But it sure can be done. Yes it can be done. Look at all the hitherto impossible things that man has done. Nothing is impossible anymore. Absolutely nothing.

The last chart belonged to a patient who had been laying in the emergency room for more than thirty-six hours. Every consult imaginable had been called with no discernible diagnosis. A difficult case. Waiting for the patient to get sicker before he could be correctly diagnosed.

8

Nothing was more rewarding than arriving to the end of a shift especially on days when everything has gone wrong. Seeing relief come was both exhilarating and rejuvenating. Except for a few chronic late comers, most attending physicians strive to come on time.

On the schedule to replace doctor Oligo was doctor Freedman. At this point every indication was that doctor Freedman is going to be late. It seemed out of place for a doctor who had earned the reputation of 'doctor punctuality'. He would rather be half an hour early than a minute late. It was now five minutes past the hour and he had not shown up. More disturbing, he had not called to let doctor Oligo know that he was running late. Patiently, doctor Oligo waited since he dared not leave the emergency room with no 'attending doctor' coverage.

Time crawled slowly. Many more patients straddled in. Some arrived on stretchers via the ambulance. Others came in accompanied on their heels by staff of emergency medical services converted to cab drivers and companions. Real to expectation there was some sort of quiet interval signaling the end of one shift and before the beginning of another shift. A sign out period.

Regular patients who understood how the system operated avoid utilizing the emergency room during this transition period. The exiting staff tended to sweep matters under the carpet so that they could go home as soon as possible. These two mix combined to artificially give a transient false sense of serenity. Very much like the calm before the storm.

Fifteen minutes had gone by and still no sign of doctor Freedman. Doctor Oligo listened intently as another set of phone began to ring. The desk clerk was answering quickly and putting the calls on hold. "Silver Greek hospital please hold. Silver Greek hospital please hold. Silver Greek hospital, please hold. Silver Greek hospital, please hold". Her method was both plastic and detached. A total of four calls were put on hold while she sorts out the pins and needles in the hay-sack of her procrastination. Her splitting migraine headache prevented her from making prompt decisions.

Fourteen years at this job had sharpened her coping skill. They called her Tan, short for Tangayika. Probably in her late thirties. She would never win a beauty contest. She did not have any need for make-up but she used them profusely anyway. No amount of facial mold could undo the disservice that nature had done to her. Layers of pancake rob off her face like the hairy body of a gifted moth. Behind those protective walls of facial mask is a troubled no nonsense debonair damsel. All the staff, especially the female staffs knew and understood that once she made the announcement about their calls it was final. No repetition. No reminder. "I am neither your boy-friend nor your private secretary" she had pointed out to the head nurse who felt slighted that she did not have the curtsey to remind her of her call.

Interviewing parents, registering patients, answering phone calls, running errands for inventories, notifying various 'health-maintenance-organizations', fending off homophobes did not sound like an easy job. Yet she was able to make time in between to inhale cigarette smoke and pop ergotamine pills.

For some unknown reasons she and doctor Oligo never got along. Their chemical aura never came to flow in any predictable harmonious rhythm.

"Line three is for the attending" she yelled in between her fisted teeth. "Thanks I will be there in a moment", doctor Oligo returned the yell.

Emergencies seldom extend to phone calls unless otherwise specified. Doctor Oligo intended to take his time. After all, his shift was being stretched beyond limit with no end at site. As he weighed whether to pick up the phone now or later a deluge of scenarios welled up his imagination.

Personal calls when he should have been gone twenty-five minutes ago? Very, very unlikely.

Perhaps doctor Freedman on the line with reasons on why he has not arrived? Not surprising. Plenty of excuses to choose from. Anything to avoid this enslavement of a job; Traffic jam across the white-stone bridge, car broke down, beaten by a stomach bug, suffering from chronic fatigue syndrome. Perhaps he did not realize he was scheduled to work today. May be he switched call with doctor Allen Greenstick. That name always brought back his palpitation. Olgo hated when doctor Greenstick was to be the person to relieve him. Even though he comes in late he brings along a fine comb to nit pick on all the endorsements. Signing out to him is like going through the pain of a thrombosed hemorrhoid. Many attending physicians avoided getting gritty with him because of his ethereal connection.

Not to be easily repressed was the hunch that it could be his wife calling for the tenth time on the hour to find out if he would be coming home alive. His wife's anxiety was the last thing on his mind at this moment. Doctor Oligo was not ready yet to give unwavering predictions of how long it was going to take him to get back home. After all these years it was her right to be the first to know all his moves before it happened, his wife had argued emphatically. He had not been able to convince her since then that the only thing predictable in life is that it would end someday. A man's mind like the highway traffics is hazardously unpredictable . It changes with every passing second. How easy it is has been to forget that they had been married for close to ten years. The predictably unpredictable challenges had kept their vows in timeless recycling motion. Scaling through all the troughs and swings of the American turbulence. From doctor Oligo's tormenting years in residency training program to his wife's years in nursing school and graduate school. Three graduations in four years. Ready-made comfort in days of sadness.

Medical treatment in days of sickness. Nursing cares in days of fatigue. Believing that from the burnt of every injustice shall rise the ashes of triumph. Believing that the distance between wellness and sickness, between sanity and insanity, between success and failure, between grace and disgrace between, life and death is nothing but an infinitesimal illusion.

It wouldn't be funny either if it was doctor Mesmere calling in the midst of the emergency room commotion to continue with the discussion concerning his methodology in medical practice.

True to his earlier promise to catch up with doctor Mesmere, the two had met in the solitude of the doctors on-call room on a quiet Sunday morning. Doctor Oligo had taken the young intern on a series of personal and ideological issues, trying to penetrate the fortress of his mind.

"Yes concerning the 'ear drilling and blood pressure' incident. Was that fetishism or what?", doctor Oligo had confronted him with no barriers.

Doctor Mesmere was taken aback. His neck and shoulders sagged an inch or two as if his atlas vertebra was going to crumble under the brutal force of a Herculean stone hoisted on his head.

"Uh, uh, I hope not", he had answered.

Then it is morbid obsession doctor Oligo quickly suggested trying to stuff words in doctor Mesmere's mouth to ameliorate the pain which his question had caused.

During the entire meeting doctor Mesmere looked terrified and depressed. Something obviously was eating him up. Something deeper than the eyes could see. He needed help.

Remorsefully, doctor Mesmere admitted that recently his clinical tendencies border peripherally on morbid apprehension. Trying under extraordinary stress to do everything impeccably without blemish.

"How would you characterize doctor Woeffry?", doctor Oligo inquired. "You can talk to me" doctor Oligo assured the visibly trembling intern.

"Over my dead body", the intern replied with a tone of finality. "This guy is ubiquitous".

Of course doctor Woeffrry had his ears to the ground. He belonged to the authorized gossip club. Doctor Mesmere feared that he would be kicked out of the residency program.

Doctor Oligo understood that morbid fear perfectly. How could he forget doctor Woeffry's frequent job termination threats, his fungal colonized five pudgy fingers that left an indelible indentation on his gluteus.

"Okay, doctor what do you think about medical abortion?", doctor Oligo continued with the rest of his informal assessment of doctor Mesmere.

Doctor Mesmere frowned on what he dubbed the flagrant willingness to play 'blood sucking Dracula' with lives of unborn babies in the name of a woman's right to chose. Haven't these abortionists heard about birth control pills and condoms?

Opposing the 'death penalty' wasn't tough for him either. Because as he succinctly puts it, "by the time justice is rendered the offenders are no longer in a murderous state of mind".

"How did you end up doing your residency program in the Bronx. It is pretty tough here isn't?, doctor Oligo had asked him.

"I never had a choice" ,doctor Mesmere answered.

"You could have gone to some other borough to do your residency", couldn't you? "There is Manhattan, Brooklyn, Long Island etc, it is a big state".

"No, they wouldn't permit me", doctor Mesmere said.

"Why wouldn't they let you?" ,doctor Oligo followed up with a direct question. You can pick out a sense of bewilderment and urgency in his voice.

"Albany", doctor Mesmere answered objectively.

"Why you and why did they restrict you to the Bronx?". doctor Oligo probed, determined to get to the route of this new information.

"It is a geographical quarantine based on race and color", doctor Mesmere had explained. Alien blacks and colored alien doctors are forced to practice in black and poor neighborhood. "Like vultures, the immigration lawyers feast on their isolated carcass".

"Interesting, Isn't" doctor Oligo hummed after he had gotten the ink of doctor Mesmere's explanation. This should not be happening doctor Oligo said with an ire of condemnation. "Where for God's sake are our dud head colleagues in the state medical licensing board drilled in the cross-section of human brain anatomy and physiology. Don't they have enough virility left in them to square up with the sharpness of the law makers tutored in the arts of evasion and subduecracy? What an insult to intellectual freedom. It is nothing short of disguised segregation. Condoned behind the hospital white walls. A sticking sore thumb in the often flounced medical camaraderie. Obviously a vestige of suppression and segregation, to ensure that this group of colored health care providers do not spill to the mainland and suburbs. The result is a system where the urban poor located hospitals burst at seams with patients while their suburb counterparts have more doctors than patients. Residency training converted to years of jail sentence and patient care reduced to patient curse. Surely, grandpa hippocrates would be nauseated if he were alive to hear this. Didn't he admonish that 'your colleagues shall be your brothers?'"

By the time doctor Oligo had done reminiscing over the events of the past few days, a phony caller supposedly would have hung up. He has been getting hundreds of such calls. Not only from angry patients who blamed him personally for all the ER ills, but also from anonymous individuals who questioned his sanity in his un-relentless effort to invent 'inspigorate'.

The caller waited. An indication that it might indeed be an important call. Doctor Oligo took the last sip of his lukewarm decaffeinated coffee, tripped the empty cup clumsily on the clerk's desk, grabbed the phone with his left hand and fought his way through the make-up smudges left by Ms. Tan.

"Hello, this is doctor Oligo speaking, very sorry you were put on hold for so long. How can I help you?" It didn't take him long time to realize from the background hubbub that this was not going to be any regular call. Noise of desperate struggles greeted his ears.

A voice emerged from the other end of the line to announce

"emergency medical service on the line". The driver seemed to be speaking from a speakerphone. A boom sound was reverberating on Oligo's end. Complete hearing was difficult but the message got through anyway.

"We are less than three minutes away from your emergency room. On board the ambulance is a seven year old male. Accidental gunshot wound to the head. Glasgow coma scale is 3. He has a tube down the trachea. We are bagging with 100% oxygen. Cardiopulmonary resuscitation is on the way. We have not had spontaneous breathing since we scooped him. No Pulse either. End tidal Carbon dioxide is 70. Lots of bleeding from the scalp wound. The field monitor is showing flat cardiac reading. Our team has administered two doses of intravenous epinephrine, a single dose of mannitol has been given for all it is worth. Fluid is on board too. We have not gotten any appreciable response yet.

The child apparently got hold of Dad's loaded gun. A tragedy that could have been prevented had there been a child's trigger safety lock." Doctor Oligo need not be a genius to figure that out himself. However, he must remain pragmatic in tackling this problem.

Between calling a code and asking for a detour to another hospital was a choice he urgently needed to make. Lamentation is the last thing going through his mind. A severely head injured child arriving to a facility with no neurosurgeon? That wasn't going to happen. They packed up their borehole drills many years ago. The new director argued successfully that there weren't enough high paying potential victims to support their trade.

Cloud of dilemmas came down from the sky to dampen his decision making faculty. A life and death decision to be thrust upon him. On his bare hands. Relying only on abrasive insensitive obsolete medical instruments. If only he had 'inspigorate'. Perhaps he could take on this case knowing that he would be able to wake him up should he die on his hand.

But he had yet to crystallize 'inspigorate' beyond the privacy of his imagination. He had not gotten the chance he craved for. Events had moved so quickly. Years had breezed passed him.

Responsibilities had piled up to the roof. Unpaid bills driving him insane. No more was he at the prime of his wits. Besides, opposition is beginning to take a toll on him. He had to deal with weird graffiti appearing every morning on his car windows, on his apartment door and on his hospital white coat. Wherever he went people followed him around with placards. They wanted him to quit and to give up his pursuit of knowledge. "Let the spirit of the dead rest in peace. Do not second-guess God. Give it up now. Go try your device on your own people in Africa". They failed to understand that he was only trying to realize a childhood dream. There would be no going back. Quitting was an act of ignorance.

But could such a device deliver where there has been substantial destruction of vital human tissue, like in a gun shot wound to the head? Probably not. Time is of essence. "Take him to Harlem center", Doctor Oligo finally said. "The patient needs an emergent neuro-surgical intervention. Continue all you are doing at the moment. I think you are on the right track. Maintain zero to minimal head movement. Keep that expired carbon dioxide trimmed a little more. Keep ventilating patient. Watch that mannitol. Give more fluid if you must to maintain euvoleamia. Remember your AB—C's of resuscitation. Airway, air, Oxygen, Oxygen, Oxygen. Breathing, Breathe, oxygen, oxygen. That is what life is. That is the oil in the automobile of life. That is the umbilical link that provides life nourishment from the creator. Do not sever it. Do not give up. Your actions can definitely prevent further brain swelling and make a difference in saving the lads life. Good luck" he added rather ominously.

They ambulance driver sensed the repulsion. He detoured as they were talking. Doctor Oligo could hear the bellowing of the full blast siren as the ambulance weaved toward a major road intersection. Their conversation tapered awhile before disconnecting, leaving doctor Oligo with a lingering curiosity. Did the hospital administration activate his earlier plea for patient diversion?

9.

Brain scramble and finger pointing is something the medical management endeavors to do at random. The direction of their sticky fingers changes depending on whose ox they want to gore. All the attending physicians, residents and moonlighters are mandated to be present. The last meeting was barely fifteen days ago. And once again the director had called for an impromptu meeting. What a medical autocrat. As usual it was a blindfolded agenda with him serving as an indispensable life time moderator.

Flanked by his sides were his old and new set of trusted tentacles; Doctor Woeffry, lady Burgh his new personal secretary and his hand pick medical biller Mr. Lanny.

Mr. Lanny had been touted as a financial wizard who could elevate a mere diagnosis of 'cold' into a life threatening encephalitis. He was given the well-deserved opportunity to speak first. He was brief and intensely excoriating. "Physicians continue to be weak in their choice of diagnosis code. This must stop forthwith. You all know how we usually get back at you. Skin shave on your paycheck, remember that. Give us what we ask of you and we shall take care of the rest". You could notice the director's concurring head nodding like the unstable top of agama lizard. After every three seconds or so he would turn his head to nod in a different direction. His message loud and clear. For the record, everybody else was asked to make a statement on how to better some of the ills infesting the emergency room in particular and the hospital in general.

Doctor Woeffry: "Some residents continue to avoid getting

rectal exam. By not sticking your hand in that hole you fail to identify hundreds of rectal and prostate cancers. More critically you make the department vulnerable to countless law suits. Money awarded to plaintiffs can run into millions of dollars. Therefore, if any resident is still not sure on how to get a good rectal exam they should come to me. Come to me baby".

The director played dumb and looked the other way, the male residents flushed with despair while the female residents shied in sympathy. Doctor Mesmere, got up, excused himself and left the meeting.

Doctor Oligo mused between talking and remaining silent. Eventually, he made a decision to speak out his concerns.

"Patients still out number the physicians in the emergency room at a ratio of 60:1" he said summarily. "We need to change that. We need to hire more doctors for the benefit of efficient medical practice. Patients are waiting too long, paying too much money for ailments that grandmothers could handle at home in a matter of second. On the flip side, he continued "a large number of patients continue to harass resident doctors. Especially female interns. Something must be done about this. A frightened doctor is as good as a spinal animal".

Midway through his speech he gazed towards the director who had positioned himself behind the high table. Their eyes collided. It was the director who backed down. Doctor Oligo noticed that the director's outstretched hand was fidgeting. His secretary dumped a face towel in it. He went with it to his face wiping feverishly. Then he stood up unannounced, cut doctor Oligo off and took a verbal whack on him. He washed him down and painted him with the brush of an outlandish outcast.

"Are you not a graduate from a third world medical school?" It was more of a statement than a question. "Yes I am", doctor Oligo concurred eager to please him. Wishing he could stop any further embarrassment. But he didn't. Nothing could stop the director in his attacking state of mind. So, doctor Oligo put on his emotional armor and braced up for the director's rage. He could tell from the director's voice that the animosity he harbored towards him took some time to build.

In front of the director was a red file jacket. He paged up and down the content. Found what he was looking for. "During your interview ten years ago with doctor Woeffry you indicated that you wanted to find a device that could reverse death?" "Yes I did", doctor Oligo answered realizing that he had been busted big time. "But I now know better" he quickly added adroitly. Warding off strangers who opposed his impending invention is one thing, but squaring against the brick hand of his employers was suicidal.

"Information reaching my desk indicates that you are far from giving up that nutty project of yours", the director countered. He glided his fingers through the file until he came to a red ribbon tagged page. "At 3:50 pm on November 7" he read, "you met with an engineer that was supposed to help fit in nuts and bolts on your fantasy. If you had such a great mind, why ask for help? Why don't you go at it alone? Two grievous charges against you doctor Oligo.

First, you are doing everything humanly possible to disturb the peaceful rest of the dead. That is outrageous enough. Whatever ideas you have can never scale over the tough litmus test set by the fat cats. For one thing, you do not have the right credentials. You are not from here, don't you realize that? You are a native of Burundu. The poorest country on earth. You can't be serious. Your ideas cannot be taken seriously, your device cannot muster the necessary greens to keep it afloat.

Secondly, and unpardonable, you are suggesting that patients no longer wait before they are seen by doctors. How many of these proposed services of yours exists where you came from?" "Hardly any in Burundu", doctor Oligo had said interrupting him again and praying he would find a final period and stop.

"What do you think I am doing here doctor Oligo, running a drive-through hamburger shop?", the director fumed. Doctor Oligo did not have other options left but to fight back and defend his childhood dream. "Let me differ with you sir, my ideas are not fantasy. It is real. It is both logical and plausible. I believe it can be done. If not by me by someone out there. Not for me but for the bereaved. For generation to come. It is worth a real trial. It is an idea I had since I was born. As far back as I can remember. Ever since my mother rescued me from the powerful jaws of death using the innocuous powers of the breath. The idea has grown with me and could no longer be hidden. It has absorbed in all my faculties of existence. I see it, I hear it, I smell it, I feel it, I breathe it. It is now ready to pop like over-inflated balloon. Nothing but success can salvage it". The director stood motionless and listened. He did not expect doctor Oligo to put on a fight in defense of his ideas.

"Well listen" the director began after regaining his composure, "all I say to you is that you have violated the letters of your contract. As long as you continue to be paid by Silver Greek hospital you shall devote your entire time to us. Including all your thoughts. Both on duty and off duty. Besides your idea would not augur well for business. No matter how you look at it everybody looses. It is a simple economic interdependence ratified by nature. If you succeed in reversing death on everybody that dies, guess what, the funeral homes would be the first to go out of business. Then there would be population explosion. The government would have more mouth to feed. Where do you think they would get the money to do that? More taxes, huh huh. Me and you would be hit so hard in the only place it matters. The bottom line"

Immediate adjournment was called following the sore dialogue between the director and doctor Oligo. He knew the fate of other doctors who had dared to tell the director how to run his job. The residents and some of the attending doctors came around to get doctor Oligo's contact address and wish him the best of luck. Like the pale victim of a vicious inoperable malignancy his days at Silver Greeks were numbered. The rest of the doctors kept pace with him to a point until everybody parted to their different destination. Soon he was left alone to ponder his destiny.

Doctor Oligo retreated into the confines of his shell to retrace his footstep down the memory lane. As always he stopped to take a look up at the gradient of the future. Reflecting on the sum total of his medical pathway. Once again, he could here the echoes of his teachers foretelling that the medical pathway was going to be a part laid with needles and sharps. The medical school graduation speech made by the dean almost twenty years ago downloaded visibly in front of him. "Failure may sometimes be inevitable", the wizardry dean had said. "But mediocrity? No, God. Never. He despised that. Not another dump in the belly of already bloated Bell curve".

The hiccup sound of the only ventilator at Burundu General hospital buzzed in his ears. The helpless face of the surgeon asking for his favorite instrument appeared from nowhere. Apparition of the medical school embryologist rattling on the genesis of human life froze the flow of blood in his veins. He felt the suckers of angry mosquitoes feeding on his blood as he conducted night rounds in his village practice in Burundu. The nightmares were unbearable. It wouldn't go away.

Doctor Oligo had always believed that he was destined to be a physician. To the extent that it never dawned on him what the societal expectations and the sacrifice were going to be. By age seventeen he was already a first year medical student, memorizing the Guyton's textbook of physiology. Arguably at that age he did not possess enough intellectual depth to fully wrap his arms around the limitations and handicap of the profession. The more knowledge he gained about life and death the more hopeless and discouraged he became. Every chapter of every severe disease ended in death. From Lupus sclerosis through amyotrophic lateral sclerosis to lung cancer, the patients ultimately succumbs. He quickly concluded that man would always die and perhaps would always remain dead when they die.

But his conclusion was short lived. As array of new information bombarded his gray cells, he escaped the entrapment of dogmatic finalities. Life, words and the world ought to be dynamic variables. And therefore acceptable standard must vary from generation to generation. That set his mind thinking again. Maybe he could garner enough wits to stretch a man's longevity to many hundreds of years. Like Methuselah who lived for over seven hundred years. That goal also proved to be a wishful thinking. So far all his childhood desires for the afflicted have fallen like a stack of dominoes. Probably this was the moment for him to accept the prevailing standard of life and death. Perhaps time has come for him to reevaluate his commitment and dedication to this profession based on reality. After all stress had rocketed rapidly. Old colleagues have turned against younger ones. The moneybags have hijacked medical decisions. Robots have learned enough medicine to make dinosaurs out of doctors. Respect had declined in leaps. Very much different from his little village of Burundu where he first laid hand on the sick. Where physicians were appreciated for the job they did. Age forty was not particularly a pubescent age anymore in this career. Constantly faced by the threat of mayhem in his everyday medical practice. Not really sure whether he was content by just alleviating only a portion of his patients affliction, which was less than a nano-decimal of his childhood dreams. He Wondered if it was time for him to pack up his stethoscope and leave town to get away from all the fiasco. To pursue something more rewarding and fulfilling. Become a historian where even the passage of time can not erase the prints of his words. Or a fiction writer with the make-believe power of resurrecting their characters when they die. Or even become one of the postmortem wall street stock analyst, who always had the right explanation no matter which way the market turns. Anything but watch helplessly while another of his patient die before his very own eyes. The convoluted thought left him no room for escape.

The intruding tap on his right shoulder put him side by side with a man he knew he had met before. A man he had hoped would bring satisfactory conclusion to his pursuit. A man he knew would provide flesh to the spirit of 'inspigorate'. And silence the disbelievers once and for all. Time may have passed by, but the flame still burned in him. Stronger than ever. His thirst had been unquenchable. Every second of every hour was worth the wait. He had learned patience from his most patient patients.

A rimmed spectacle. A sealed lip. A blank face. That could only be one person, the engineer. Every other thing about him had changed. The jet black hair replaced by brittle kinky hair. A narrow thin face replaced by a coarse desperate one. The high profile 'T' shirt had gone too. Replacing it is a faded no-name dress-down shirt. In place of spotless black leather jacket was a brown worn out coat. He looked as if he had been dug out from a pile of animal dung. His lopsided boots winced out in defiance as he trounced mercilessly in them. A puffed up brief case weighed heavily on his left shoulder.

He had spotted Oligo first and beckoned on the doctor to join him at the adjacent coffee shop. Doctor Oligo was ecstatic to join him. It was a dream come true. Unexpectedly the angels were in tandem with his aspiration. How else would you like to explain the reappearance of the engineer. Every leap in human elevation has been a product of accidental spontaneous reorganization. He let his entropy flow victoriously. His stiff white coat against the background of the engineer's ramshackle clothes attracted the snoopy eyes of hungry diners. The two found a secluded spot at the back corner, and sat opposite each other across a McDonald sized table. An observant Spanish waitress hopped to take their orders.

"Coffee", the engineer said in a low key voice.

"Same for me" doctor Oligo added rather hurriedly.

Minimum order? The waitress loitered around for more orders. None was forthcoming. Only two cups of coffee? Less than a buck and a half. She wasn't quite sure if that would generate a tip afterwards. So she left. Another unsuspecting male waiter came forward to fill the orders.

The engineer unloaded half of the content of his handbag to rescue it from respiratory compromise. He set them in two uneven piles, leaving a hand print of mud and hay on top. Finally the inertia waned and his lips unzipped.

"You do recognize me?"

"Yes of course", doctor Oligo answered. "How in the world could I forget", doctor Oligo reassured him. "We met six months ago. Designer engineer of 'Current de-Generale. I have been looking out for you ever since we parted".

The interrupting overhead announcement was unnervingly

unmistakable. "Code Blue adult ER". "Code blue adult ER"—The multiple repetition was embarrassingly annoying. Attracting anybody and anything that had to do with patient care.

The missing house cleaner had suddenly reemerged, resting his foot on the crash cart. The auxiliary hospital cook abandoned her breakfast cart to glue herself to the patient's monitor screen. The administrator and the medical biller kept their mouth on the nursing drug sheet recalculating medical expenditure and balancing out hospital gains versus wastes. The hospital chaplain waited impatiently on his wings to administer the last sacrament. The cops, the firefighters, and the ambulance personnel all refused to give up ground on their occupied territories.

By the time doctor Oligo flew back to the emergency room, 'CPR' had been well on the way. He fought his way through the human barricade to reclaim his rightful position close to the patient. "The attending, please give way. The ER attending, please step aside. The attending please—.You have done 'CPR' for a minute, now give the first dose of epinephrine", doctor Oligo commanded. The nurse literally wrestled the medication book from the medical biller to chart the doctor's order. "Could you excuse me?", doctor Oligo said to the cook who remained transfixed to the patient's monitor. The cook drew a string of sigh before she hesitantly stepped aside.

Finally doctor Oligo got the opportunity to see the cardiac monitor. "Ventricular fibrillation", doctor Oligo bemoaned. "Get ready for shock". Everybody cleared. 200joules of shock was delivered via the defibrillator. The patients lifeless body jerked up and down. "No change in patient's condition. Continue CPR", doctor Oligo declared. "One minute is up, give another epinephrine" he continued, following the dictates of the medical code drill.

The timekeeper summed the time passed since the beginning of the resuscitative effort to be a little over thirty minutes. Doctor Oligo could visualize oxygen molecules fleeing from the patient's body cells and exiting through the wide open mouth. It was a cascading phenomena clearly revealed by the patient's continuous gasps of breathe.

"Maybe the Engineer came along with 'inspigorate", doctor Oligo wished desperately. What else could have been in the puffy bag. He stifled the temptation to abscond from the patient's bedside to conclude his meeting with the engineer. Doctor Oligo knew that with 'inspigorate' he could reverse the prevailing event and completely change the outcome. But with out inspigorate his patient was going to succumb to death. There would be no getting around it. Situation was dire. He knew it. The code team knew it. They just wouldn't admit it. Forty five minutes down the stretch , they were still thumping on the victims chest.

Then a moment later the patient's heart beat came to a screeching halt. The cardiac monitor drew a long flat line indicating absence of electrical activity of the heart. The flat line continued unabated. Another exercise in futility. Absolutely nothing to show for it. Other than the money made by the hospital management.

"Close to a quarter million?" The administrator inquired stroking his thin greedy moustache. "Yeah", the medical biller assured him with a wink of his moth-eaten eyelash. "Very close, we see". They both chuckled.

The patient's bedside was now deserted. Left only to the chaplain. He seemed to be having problem convincing the mother of the deceased.

"I know that Jerald is in heaven with the angels" the chaplain assured the mother.

"But I needed him" the mother cried out. "He is all I have. My life would be over without him. Please do something. Ask God to bring him back".

"God knows the best, the very best" the chaplain added, rather redundantly.

"I heard of a doctor working on a project that would reverse death. Get him, maybe he could help" the woman begged.

"I am not sure the doctrine would allow that. Every soul that parted with its body must stand before the almighty for judgment. Trust me on that" the chaplain concluded.

The nurse attendant returned to get the deceased ready for

the morgue. The resident doctors feverishly scribbled their notes in a special way to make sure the lawyers are kept off the case. They went over their notes repeatedly. Crossed their 'T's and dotted their 'I's.

Doctor Oligo could not take the scenario anymore. He headed back to the coffee shop to find the engineer. He took a couple of steps forward but was check-mated by Randy, the chaplain.

"You tried your very best, didn't you?" ,the reverend reassured doctor Olgo. "Now what is the talk about this invention of yours that would make eternal life optional".

"Let me go. Let go of my hands. I have to go", doctor Oligo protested. There wasn't anytime left for him to lose focus. Talking frivolities wouldn't do him any good. A five minute session with the engineer was all he needed to settle this matter once and for all. He is not prepared to let it slip by. The jigsaw puzzle had finally come together. The engineer was ready. His job days were numbered. Good time for him to seize the moment and follow his destiny.

"What was it all about?", the engineer asked inquisitively.

"I lost another of my patients" the doctor replied. "All because of you and your greedy company. You wasted so much time. Now where is 'inspigorate'? Did you do it? Do you have good news for me? Common dig into your bag and show me the prototype. Please tell me you have it in your bag". Doctor Oligo's impatience was hysterical.

The engineer stared at his bag for a brief moment. Lifted it to the intimacy of his left lap. Unzipped the side compartment. Then hesitated and paused. Turned a subdued gaze at doctor Oligo. His eye balls set to sail into a pendulous movement by the drowning tears. Frustration choking his throat. He struggled to let the words out. "They wouldn't let me complete the job", he muttered.

"Who? Who wouldn't let you", doctor Oligo interrogated him, visibly frustrated. The engineer ignored him. He obviously had a mind of his own. Instead, he retrieved clipped sheets of paper from his folder and dumped it on doctor Oligo's face. "Look here", he said pointing acid chopped fingernails through endless logarithm of mathematical and technical drawing. "The sum total of all the technical linkages equals zero, he explained to doctor Oligo. The zero is synonymous with life perpetuity. If the mysterious breathe that went in at birth is recaptured and fed into the body every time it exited from it then there was no energy lost and the sum total of the primordial gas exchange would be zero. I knew I had it. I had it. I got the soul of it. The engineer was literally thumping on his pectus carinatum". He geared up and continued again. "I only needed to wrap the soul in a sheet of metallic matter, which by the way is simpler. But they threw me out, he said with an ire of forlorn exasperation. A fish thrown out of water has no chance of surviving. That is what they did to me. My company did that. They accused me of devoting too much time on the project. It seemed to me that nobody wanted to see the dead man walk again. The biggies, the government, the churches. Movements for the protection of the dead. Heir apparent right groups. They all sprang up on me. They can't accept it. They can't take it. Take it from me, time is not ripe to complete the project. Be patient".

"But when is time gonna be ready?", Doctor Oligo countered, visibly enraged. "Lets carry on just for the sake of the bereaved. Geeve me what you got. Geeve that to me, I would take it from there". Doctor Oligo matched his protest by clutching on one end of the blueprint.

"You need a sponsor, the cost to put clothes on that baby is staggering", the engineer reminded him.

Never mind, I would find a sponsor, whatever it takes, doctor Oligo responded.

The two were creating quite a scenario as they held each end of the long sheet of the blueprint in a tug of war. They were getting noticed and fleas of people slowed to eavesdrop on them.

Doctor Oligo turned to inspect the spectators. The tangential beam coming from his eyes settled on the medical director's larva boring eyes. Oligo squinted and redirected his eye beam by sixty or so angle. The hospital chaplain came into focus, his eyes had the looks of a fallen spring leave.

Two of his most toxic detractors had conspired to stop him. Once again he found himself making a quick decision. He would let the engineer retain the blueprint. This certainly would be the time for him to vacate the stage. Drop out from the race of human intellectual double standard. He made quick declining steps across the six steep stairs that led to the ambulance base. Suddenly there was an uproar of siren. A dying man is about to be rushed in to the ER. Does he stand a chance? All the other motorist were on stand still.

As he walks away an inner recorded voice appealed repeatedly to him. "Time will never be ready. Go ahead and do it. Just for the bereaved".